Twisted Star

The Twisted Realms Series Book Three

Megan Guilliams

Dark Moon Rising Publications | Virginia

70 Foxwood Drive

Rocky Mount, Virginia24151

Tel: (540) 257-2861

ISBN: 978-1-972596-00-5

10 9 8 7 6 5 4 3 2 1

Printed in the United States of America

Twisted Star

PROLOGUE

Lark Henson loved to drive down to the edge of town, taking her laptop with her, and venture to the mountain. There, she would sit under the age-old weeping willow and write some of her best stuff. That is what the woman did for a living: she wrote fantasy-horror books that almost seemed to fly off the shelves the minute they were printed. She was able to make a rather good living at what she did, too, but all of that came to a halt very recently.

Lark had never been one to be pressured into deadlines. She always thought they stifled the creativity that made some of her books amazing. Unfortunately, the company she was contracted to decided to take on a new business partner... Richmond Hayes and the man couldn't care less about creativity; he wanted profits.

"Listen here, Lark. You're the best writer in this building. Hell, you might be the best writer in the state. It honestly doesn't matter to me, though. I'm only interested in how we will make a profit come the second quarter, and you've been sitting on this book." Richmond looked at the paper in his left hand and let out a little scoff. "Lark, you've been sitting on this thing for months. If you wait too long, you'll lose your fan base. I need a first draft on my desk by the end of the month." Lark couldn't help but roll her eyes at the man. He had clearly never written a memo, much less a novel. Getting up from her desk, she walked over to the man and pulled the paper from his hand. Sitting it gently on the table, she tilted her head to one side and tried to look friendly.

"With all due respect, Mr. Hayes, I can try my best, but I never do well with deadlines. This might put a rather bad crutch on me."

"I don't care what you have to do to finish this, this... What was the title of your novel again?" Richmond looked down at the paper on the table and smirked. "Rise of the willow tree? What kind of name is that?" Again, Lark tried her best not to scowl at the man in the brown suit, but she felt like she may have been just a little.

"It's the third book, Mr. Hayes. I'm reviving some of the old characters; that's why it's taking so long. It has to be perfect. My readers would eat us alive if it weren't." Motioning for Lark to go back to her seat, she nodded and returned to the computer screen that had been blinking at the words CHAPTER ONE all morning. Richmond had no idea that the woman had been struggling with this book for exactly four months and hadn't written a single word.

"Maybe getting out of the stuffy office would get the old creative juices flowing," Richmond said as he began to walk away from her desk. "Why don't you work from home for a while?"

Snatching her little blue laptop, Lark wasted no time leaving the building and jumping into her green car. She couldn't take the pressure this new partnership put her under. Along with this ridiculous writer's block, she knew she had to escape for a while. Driving back to her house, she mulled over ideas about how to get herself writing again. She could think of nothing until she got a phone call that night at dinner time.

"Why don't you stay with me for a few days? I have the whole week off and have some good things planned out. Tomorrow, I was gonna go on a hike up Old Beast Mountain. I was gonna go alone, but it would be more fun with a partner." Lark leaned against the bar beside the sink in her kitchen. She hadn't seen Shelby in a long time, even though Shelby had just lived one town over in Coral Bay.

The two girls had met in second grade, and even though they were vastly different, they hit it off immediately. Shelby Willton was a go-getter; if there was something she wanted, she would fight until she got it. Growing up, she always had the boys following her around like puppies. It didn't help that she had long, curly blond hair that framed her perfect, pear-shaped face, and when she smiled, she had deep dimples placed perfectly in the center of each of her cheeks. Lark had always thought it funny that she could have had any boy in town, but didn't bother dating. Not even in high school.

Lark was the quiet and reserved type in school. One that everyone forgot about, and that was alright with her. She loved spending quiet evenings at the library or at her house, reading books and watching old movies. She was probably just as pretty as Shelby, but in a less conventional sense. She had shorter red hair and wild green eyes that seemed to dart around the room. They were set wide on her face, so they gave her an almost alien type of look. She had a crooked smile that had its own charm and a thin frame.

The following day, Lark packed a few of her belongings and the dreaded laptop that loomed over her head like a prison sentence and drove to the tiny town of Coral Bay. She hadn't been there since she was a child, but things hadn't changed much. The old bread factory at the edge of town had burned to the ground a few years ago, and she passed it driving through. No one ever really knew for sure what had happened.

It was right before Halloween, and the factory had worked overtime to get the holiday orders in. Most people thought there must have been an electrical fire, but the conspiracy nuts all thought the same thing: that the weird little girl with the scar on her cheek had lit the place up.

It was true that weird things happened that year, and the toxic runoff had caused things to mutate in the swamp, but the local FDA and HAZMAT teams had put an end to all of that… or at least Lark thought she had heard something like that on the news a while back. No one with common sense went out into the woods and down to the swamp. Better safe than sorry!

It was good that Shelby didn't want to go for a wilderness hike and only wanted to scale Beast Mountain. Lark had also heard a few things about that place, but the stories eluded her mind for some reason. It was for the best, she thought as she pulled up to the quaint little white single-story house that belonged to her friend.

Turning off the car engine, Lark looked over just in time to see Shelby emerge from the open front door. She had on a large floppy hat, and she was wearing gloves. Lark figured she had been out back, tinkering in her flower bed. Shelby loved nature and took great care and pride in her garden.

"Long time no see, partner!" Lark said as she exited the car, lugging a little pink suitcase and a backpack. Shelby came over to greet her and took the suitcase from her hands.

"Come in!" She said, motioning to the house. Shelby was beaming ear to ear with the excitement of seeing her friend after so long. She rarely got visitors, what with the town's history; hell, more than likely, that was why Lark's family had moved away when she was in the fifth grade. They had rekindled their friendship in college, but after graduation, Shelby moved back here with her Master's in Environmental Science. Lark moved to the larger town of Shadows End with her degree in Literature. It wasn't long before Shelby saw Lark Henson's name everywhere. The small town was buzzing about how the local girl made it big time in the writing business, and Shelby figured she was too busy for visits until she called with this writer's block issue. And Shelby took the opportunity to get her back into town.

Once the girls had settled in and Shelby had started dinner, the two sat down at the kitchen table to hash out the details of the climb.

"So, tell me about this Beast Mountain," Lark said as she leaned closer. She wanted to pay close attention to what Shelby had to say. Lark might have been the writer at the table, but Shelby was known to spin a surprisingly good web herself. Maybe an old legend would get the gears going, and Lark could write a little something before bed.

"Well, Beast Mountain is the mountain that connects the five converging little towns. Coral Bay," Shelby lifted her hand like a game show girl, and Lark let out a little snort. Shelby smiled and continued with her story, "Your new hometown, Shadows End, Finch Hollow, that's the town on the other side of us, Crimson Ridge, and, of course, who could forget the wonderful township of Eagles Nest? The Mountain got its name from its sheer size. Some people also thought they saw smoke coming from it long ago, and now we wonder if it's an inactive volcano."

"Does it have any cool origin stories? I need some inspiration for this book I'm writing. Richmond is on my ass." Shelby got to her feet and walked over to the stove top, where the two girls could smell the stew beginning to boil. Lark's mouth was watering. Shelby must be an excellent cook. Taking the lid off the boiling pot, Shelby began stirring the soup with a wooden spoon.

"I don't know." She said in a sing-song voice that Lark knew was just for effect. "You might not want to go up if I tell you some of the things that allegedly happened there."

"Pleeeeeeeaaaaase." Lark pleaded as she put her hands together in front of her like she was praying. "You're my only hope!" Putting the spoon back down and placing the top on the stew pot, Shelby put a hand on her hip and looked at her friend.

"Fine, I guess. But!" Shelby pointed a finger at Lark as she returned to the table to sit down. "You have got to promise me that you will still go tomorrow. A little exercise and fresh air will help you much more than some dusty old legends."

"I promise!" Lark said eagerly and leaned in again to listen to what Shelby had to say.

"Well, a long time ago, this whole area here was a little village with noble people and elders and all kinds of cool shit that I wished still existed. On the top of Beast Mountain, there was this cool stone castle. I don't know the whole story, but if you really want to know about it, we could go to the library and read about it. Anyway, legend has it that two sisters were born up there, and it caused this big old fuss cause one of them was white as snow and couldn't come out except at night, and, back then, everyone thought if you weren't the same as them, you were a witch or something." Lark snorted, laughing again, and ran her hands through her short red hair.

"Witches? You're going to talk to me about mythical and perfectly unrealistic creatures like witches?"

"Hey, now!" Shelby said with a grin. "I thought you wanted to hear about the mountain."

"Well, yeah, but you know real stuff," Lark said; her attention had waned, and she had sat back in the chair.

"It's a fun story; they said it started some kind of uprising, and the fairy folk wanted them both dead."

"You don't believe this stuff, do you?" Lark said, rolling her eyes.

"No," Shelby said with a grin. "But, if you hear the sound of bells when the sun begins to set behind the mountain, you'd best be wary. That's the sound of the man-eating Fairy."

CHAPTER ONE

Richmond had been pacing the floor of his office, waiting for the phone to ring, but it had not done so.

"What are you waiting for!" He said, pointing a finger at the silent line. The phone rang almost as if on cue, and Richmond leaped over the desk to pick it up on the first ring.

"Hello?" He said with a stammer. He knew that time was of the essence, and Lark had taken the bait, just like he knew she would. Deadlines were the girl's worst enemy; getting her back to Coral

Bay was the most important thing he could do for the company. They had been waiting for the timing to be perfect, and the two girls together were a perfect storm. One that would bring back someone particularly important to Richmond.

"She's with Willton now; they are in the house." Richmond let out a sigh of relief. Lark hadn't backed out, which was a step in the right direction. "This better go how you say it will, Hayes, or it's your skin... Literally." The voice on the other end of the line said in a deep, raspy voice. Richmond had never met the man in person, but anyone who had told the man not to cross Victor Zanborn.

Victor wasn't born into the Guild of Magics. He had worked his way up to the top of the pyramid and knew what he was talking about regarding prophecies. Just a few months ago, Richmond got the green light to infiltrate this company and discover everything he could about Lark Henson. There wasn't much to read, and what he could find wasn't exactly exciting stuff. That's why Hayes was so surprised when Zanborn called and told him that she was extremely important to the guild and that he had to find a way to get her back to her hometown. Lark had to be there by a certain day, and she needed to climb Beast Mountain.

At first, Richmond couldn't think of a clever way to trick her into going to Coral Bay. The town didn't have a very pleasant history, but then the idea struck him that her childhood friend lived there, and with the threat of a deadline looming over her head, a simple phone call would have done the trick.

The night before Richmond dropped the bombshell on the girl, he made a phone call to the guild, explaining the situation.

"I think I have just the man for the job." The woman on the other side of the phone said. She had a smooth and sensual voice; Richmond could listen to her all day. "Stardock, his name is Stardock, and he will call you once the job is completed." The line went dead, and Richmond returned the phone to its cradle. What kind of name was Stardock anyway? Who cared as long as he got the job done?

It was almost three in the morning when the phone began to ring at the Hayes residence. Richmond got to his feet and put on his house slippers, rubbing his eyes as he made his way to the phone in his office.

Richmond lived alone, and for good reason. His life had no place for a Mrs. Hayes, and as far as Richmond could tell, it would remain that way for the near future.

"Hello?" Richmond said as he waited for the person on the other line to respond. At first, he thought no one was there or that they had been disconnected, but after what felt like a million years, a soft-spoken voice came through the phone line.

"This is Stardock; what you have asked of me is done. The ball is in your court now." Again, the phone line on the other end went dead, and Richmond retired for the evening. As he drifted off to sleep, he couldn't help but wonder what the weird person on the other line had done. He assumed it was none of his business, but he still had to wonder.

Stardock had spent the better part of a century living among the humans. Once Hope had rid him of the fairy curse, he thought that he would be able to live a normal life, but that was just a pipe dream. After the fairy revelation happened, the ones who had survived created a Guild. Inside that guild held the mysteries and the answers to all magics and what to expect if they were ever to return, or so they thought. Elder Williams was in charge of the library and memorizing or adding to its contents. Buck Jersey, one of the best gunslingers Stardock had ever seen, was in charge of rallying the troops and teaching them to fight, make traps, and survive in treacherous lands. Molly, only being a child at the time, became quite attached to Buck, and for lack of a better word, Buck essentially adopted the girl. When he was away, Stardock took care of her like an uncle. He watched her grow and blossom into a beautiful woman. Eventually, right before she was to go to college, she ran off with a local boy and married. Stardock often thought about her, especially on nights like tonight.

He had to wait until the sun had set completely before he dared to venture out into the night. Not only because he didn't want to be seen but because the curse that made him what he was had begun to return, and the sun would burn him like fire if he weren't too careful. He both hated and enjoyed being a halfling again. He didn't like that his human features were beginning to fade, that his skin had started to wither and turn grey, and that his eyes, the blue ones, were now fading back into the black, inky marbles that allowed him to see in the dark.

He didn't mind, however, that his speed and strength had returned. Most importantly, though, the Guild's most wanted power from the half-fairy was the power of suggestion. It was a gift that he had been granted by the magic tree when he was incredibly young because he had no real home. Humans and fairies alike wanted the abomination dead; that was until the Guild was made, and for the first time, Stardock felt as though he had a family of his own.

Flitting through the backyard of Shelby's house, he couldn't help but admire her flowers. Impatience, tiger lilies, and yellow roses, all in perfect rows, lined either side of the walk she had made out of granite stones. Good thing she didn't like bluebells and morning glories, and she chose stone instead of rod iron for her walk, or the halfling would have had a hell of a time getting into the house.

It was almost serendipitous that the girl would have left the window to the kitchen open, but there it was, just like an invitation. Stardock walked in as quietly as a mouse and went to Shelby's room. The moon outside cast movement throughout the house, purple and pink dancing shadows that reminded him of the old days and the castle. They reminded him of Hope, of her beauty and her sacrifice. Things around these parts would have been much different without her and her sister.

He could hear the girl in the other room. She had a slight snore, and he could tell she was in the throes of heavy sleep. As he slipped through the cracked door, he looked at the girl. The curtain by her bedroom window had been left open, and the moonlight flooded her room with romantic light, accentuating the shimmer of her golden locks.

Stardock's eyes widened as he got closer to the woman. No, no, this couldn't be! He couldn't help but get closer to her to investigate every inch of her face as she lay slumbering. How could this be?

The woman's high cheekbones and golden locks, her broad shoulders, and sun-kissed skin, was this a descendant of the Southpaws family line? Of course not! There was no way they all died... Or did they? It was well known that the Nobleman Henry had been placed in a cell and taken care of in his final years; somewhere on the eastern side, Stardock knew, some town or village called Crimson Ridge he had visited before. Was the child Henry's? It would have been impossible to say, though Stardock wouldn't rule it out.

Slipping into the bed with Shelby, the halfling gently pushed her hair away from her ear. He leaned in as far as he could without disturbing the woman. Her smell was intoxicating, and it was all he could do not to try to bite her. His newfound taste for human flesh had become a bit of a problem, and weaning himself back onto animals was proving more difficult than he had first imagined. No wonder the people of Coral Bay had found it hard to believe he wouldn't eat them up.

"You miss your friend Lark Henson; she needs to visit you. You will not take no for an answer." Stardock had to lick his lips and swallow hard to avoid drooling on the poor girl. Shelby smiled and nodded.

"Lark." She muttered under her breath, inhaling, drinking in the cool night air.

"You and Lark need to climb Beast Mountain; you need to because there is something up there that has been waiting far too long for her, something good." Again, Shelby nodded and rolled over onto her other side; Stardock took a moment to slip back onto the bedroom floor.

"I need to climb the mountain, major surprise, happy... Lark." Shelby said as she stuck her hands under her chin. Stardock knew that his work there had been completed, and he snuck back to the open window in the kitchen, but once he had exited, he thought he should lock it. Who knows, maybe Shelby was more important than anyone else thought, but either way, the halfling would keep a close eye on the girls in case they needed his help.

CHAPTER TWO

Coral Bay had a bad habit of starting trouble. The town didn't want to, but most of the time, it wasn't really up to the town, and the people from the surrounding towns didn't usually want anything to do with its shenanigans. Tonight would be no different because after the sun had set, Misty knew that those awful grey man-eaters would start to flank her cabin.

She had thought that the mud zombies were bad enough, but a bunch of men in bio-hazard suits had eliminated that threat and the toxic radiation that had almost destroyed the town just a few years ago. No one thanked Misty for getting rid of the factory, not a single person thanked her for getting rid of not one but TWO serial killers that had been roaming free for quite a while, and certainly no one thanked her for getting rid of two of the most, wealthy men in the town that had made it so easy for the bakery to keep going. What did Misty get for all her challenging work? A warrant for her arrest! Arson, murder, and a slew of breaking and entering charges.

Misty only returned to the cabin when she knew it was safe. Usually, it was at dusk, but lately she had been going earlier. The first night she encountered these monsters, she had no idea where they had come from, but Misty took care of them as she did with any troublemaking creature. Killing came quite easy for the girl; she had been doing it for years, and after that night with Star and Lucky, she almost craved the challenge, the thrill of the fight, and these things were the first creatures to challenge her the way they did. Reaching up to her face, Misty touched the large rope scar that wrapped her cheek. It twisted and widened, stopping at the base of her ear.

It was her favorite scar. No other night of killing had ever been so much fun. Walking over to her oil lamps, the girl lit them individually, but what was inside didn't look like lamp oil. What was inside it looked black and thick, like tar, but when the girl lit the wick, it caught fire quickly and fiercely. Misty smiled as she looked down at the blue flame that danced and wiggled, casting dark, long, and dreadful shadows around the old cabin.

Misty had found out that the angry, flying mole rats that plagued her swamp had thick blood that was highly flammable. She figured that's why they burst into flames when dragged out into direct sunlight. They were highly cunning and quite silent when they wanted to be, saved for the jingling of bells. Misty couldn't for the life of her figure out why she heard the bells or if anyone else heard them when those things were close, but she had every intention of leaving first thing in the morning and visiting the library in Finch Hollow... Who knows, maybe she would visit an old friend while she was there, too? He was, after all, in prison, and she knew he wouldn't be going anywhere for a long time.

It didn't take long after Misty lit the last lamp that she heard the sounds of bells all around the house. It was good that she had done some repairs to the place, or the little grey boogers would have easily been able to get in through the ceiling or the floor. The cabin had been in disarray, but it held fond memories for the girl; honestly, she had never felt more at home anywhere else. This is where her friends were and where she would stay.

"Why won't you come play with us, little girl?" The first voice said. It sounded familiar, and Misty thought it might have been the one that got away the night before.

"Ha-ha!" Misty scoffed as she pulled gardening shears out from under her old, musty cot and made her way to the side of the front door. "You think that's gonna work on me, you little fuckers! If you want me, you're gonna have to come inside and take what you want... That is, if you have the guts." Leaning against the door, Misty waited for a few seconds. She couldn't hear anything but knew better than to pop her head out.

Again, she heard the jingling of bells, only this time, it sounded like it was coming from the bathroom. Venturing away from the front door, Misty lifted the gardening shears in front of her face, waiting for an attack. It wouldn't be the first time one of those things got in here, and Misty couldn't figure out how they were doing it.

"Good to be home." The voice cooed, and Misty could tell it was in her bathroom. The voice echoed all around the walls. Was it in the tub? She couldn't tell. Taking small steps inside the bathroom, Misty's eyes darted around strategically; she had to see it before it saw her. Long screeching sounds made their way into the girl's ears, like nails on a chalkboard, almost making her drop her shears. It made her head throb with pain, and the girl let out a little squeak.

"Get the hell out of here before I cut your ugly head off like I did to your little buddies last night." Misty hissed. She knew the little thing was hiding in the tub, running its long, black, hooked claws up and down the porcelain. The creature did not attempt to hide where he was; jumping from the tub, the monster tilted his head and smiled a thin-lipped smile, taking a step closer to the girl, but she held her shears out in front of her, ready to take the creature's life. He didn't seem too threatened by her actions, and his smile only got bigger, and he let out a little snort. He had a beaked nose pointing down to the floor and two little black beady eyes resembling marbles. His arms were a little too long for his body, almost like a gorilla, but he had no hair. Two brown, bat-like wings were perched between his shoulder blades. His feet were large, with gnarled toes that pointed in all directions. Misty thought she could smell death coming from the thing. After all, she knew that smell all too well. She could have been mistaken, though, because the swamp always had a sort of dead way about it. Another reason she loved it here.

"You have to excuse my siblings. You see, we've been asleep for an exceptionally long time, and when we wake up, we tend to be very hungry." The monster's smile grew even larger as he tilted his head to the other side.

"What the hell are you?" Misty asked and snapped her shears at the thing to prove she would, in fact, use the shears to end the trivial monster's life if needed.

"You don't know?" It asked. The sound of astonishment echoed in his words. "I thought all humans knew about the fairies. How else would you know how to protect yourself?" The fairy squatted down and put his elbows on his knees, resting his large head upon his hands.

"Do all of you eat humans?" Misty asked as she returned to the bathroom. There was a lot more room to fight in the living room; from her experience, she would need all the room she could get to best this beast.

"We're supposed to, but I've talked to my kinfolk, and we are willing to make an exception... For you."

"What is that supposed to mean?" Misty said again. She didn't want to take her eyes off the monster. They were tricky, fast, and deadly.

"My name is Deaththorne, and we have heard of you. The fairy folk think you would be an excellent family addition." Deaththorne swallowed a little hard after he said the word family, and Misty smiled at the little grey man.

"You don't have to call me family. I hated mine, so I killed them. You must not have heard as much about me as you first thought."

"No," Deaththorne continued, "That is exactly why we want you. We are well known for doing the same thing. We have no emotions save for lust, food, and power, and that is all you desire as well... And deserve. Am I not correct?" Misty put the sheers down and tilted her hip to one side.

"What's your deal? What is it you want from me? How will I know that the others will listen to you?" Deaththorne stood back up and took another step closer to the girl, but for some reason, she didn't feel as nervous as she had before.

"They will listen to everything I tell them to do; we are few; you've taken out half of my army as it is. All will be forgiven, and you can live out the rest of your life right here in this swamp if you want, with roots to unlimited power. We will protect you, but you must do something for me."

"And what is that?" Misty asked.

"I am the King of the fairies, but I have to bring back my queen. I can show you where she perished; there is a way to bring her back for good; you need a few things first, though."

"Alright, I'm listening," Misty said as she sat on the cot. The little man followed her over, and she allowed him to get closer.

"The blood of the damned, Starshallow Flowers, a very specific red stone called the Mother's heart, and a wand fashioned from the mother tree herself."

"How am I going to get all of that?" Misty said, putting her hands up in the air with exasperation. Sure, she had been able to get a hold of C4, kill zombies, and live off toxic land, but where would she get any of the things this creature spoke of?

"We will help, but when the time is right, you will have to do what you love the most... Kill," Misty smiled and nodded her head.

"Hell, if you point me in the right direction, I'm down for a little chaos. It's been quiet around here since the dead stopped talking to me."

CHAPTER THREE

Lark woke up in the middle of the night. She had been having the weirdest dream. In it, someone was chasing her. She couldn't see their face, but she knew she was frightened and that if this person caught up to her, she would most certainly die. Paired with the thought of Beast Mountain and the hidden killer dream, Lark thought it was as good a time as any to try and write the book she had been putting off for months.

Slipping out of the guest room, the girl took her laptop out of her backpack and made her way to the kitchen. She didn't want to wake her friend in the room across from hers, so she tried to do all this without turning on any lights. She reached the kitchen without incident and plugged her little computer into the wall outlet closest to the kitchen table. When she opened the top, she was bathed in the light of the computer screen. Carrying it over to the table, she sat down and began to write.

She couldn't believe she had gotten a single word out, let alone three chapters, but there she was three hours later with a particularly good start on what she had deemed the impossible book. Closing her laptop, Lark looked over at the stove clock and realized that it was almost five in the morning, and Shelby would be up soon. Lark decided to leave her computer there and get ready for the day's hike. What was the point of going back to sleep for another hour?

Getting to her feet, Lark made her way across the room but stopped at the window over the sink. She thought for just a second that there was someone out there. She could feel eyes on her and a small silhouette of someone... or something, looming under the tree just across from Shelby's garden. Taking a step closer and realizing the creature's odd shape and posture by the tree, she convinced herself it had to be a garden gnome. She let a sigh of relief escape her lips, but wanted to take it back when the little shape vanished behind the tree, and just for a second, Lark thought she heard the sound of bells jingling in the distance.

"How much longer till we get to the dreaded beast mountain?" Lark said as she rolled down the window, sitting in the passenger seat of Shelby's car.

"Not too much longer. I hope you don't mind, but I invited a friend. He loves to do stuff like this and might be a fan of yours."

"Shelby, are you trying to set me up with someone?" Shelby smirked a little and slipped her sunglasses on. Lark figured it was to avoid eye contact. She could never keep a straight face when she was lying to Lark.

"Why would you think that? If you two hit it off, that's cool, but that wasn't my intention." Rolling her eyes at her friend, Lark leaned her head out of the window and took in the beautiful countryside. She had forgotten how pretty Coral Bay really was. This one had the most fields and valleys out of all the little towns. Great for hiking and camping. Lark figured that's why Shelby never left. She loved nature so much that moving to Shadows End would have been a horrible mistake.

Lark saw an old yellow beater parked at the base of the mountain as they parked beside it.

"Hunter!" Shelby said as she jumped out of the car and ran towards her friend, throwing her arms around his neck. Hunter smiled and hugged her back. "This is my friend Lark Henson; you know the girl I told you about? She's going to be staying here for about a week." Hunter held out his hand as Lark approached.

"Hi, I'm Hunter Williams. Nice to meet you." Lark shook the man's hand and looked at Shelby with a bit of a glare. He was, in fact, her type. Tall and broad-shouldered with wavy brown hair. She knew immediately that Shelby had lied about him loving the outdoors because the man barely had a tan. He had deep-set hazel eyes and a crooked smile that made it hard not to smile back.

"I heard you liked to climb and hike," Lark said, shifting her feet back and forth. Shelby had returned to the car to get the gear out of the trunk and leave them alone for a little bit. Shelby wasn't the type of person to play matchmaker, but she had met Hunter right after the incident at Eagle's Nest. He was somewhat of a local celebrity at that time. About a year had passed since all of that had happened, and the hype had slowed down quite a bit. Shelby doubted that Lark had heard about what had happened; hell, no one except for the people there that day knew, and all of them had tight lips.

That was one of the reasons Shelby wanted to climb to the top of the mountain. It would have been easier for her to access the three-story cabin if she had just driven to Eagle's Nest and hiked up the road that had been made, but the new owners had put up giant electrical fences, so it was all but impossible to get to. If she could get to the top of the mountain from this side, she could walk right over to it undisturbed.

"I don't know about all of that," Hunter said as he put his hands in his pockets. "I used to climb in college, but that was a few years ago."

"Yeah, I'm not much of an outdoors type girl myself, but I'm working on this book, and Shelby thought that the fresh air and exercise would do me some good. You know, get the old gears going."

"Writer's block?" Hunter asked as he began to walk over to Shelby's car, helping her unload.

"Well, I thought so, but last night, I had the weirdest dream and ended up knocking out the first three chapters. "I hope the worst of it is over." Lark followed Hunter to the car, and they all geared themselves up for the long climb ahead of them.

Fortunately for the two novice climbers, the mountain wasn't as steep as it had first appeared. Of course, the three of them had tethered themselves to each other and were using hand hooks to keep their balance, but other than that, the climb was rather easy. Shelby had taken the lead, letting Lark and Hunter linger behind.

"Is this something she does a lot?" Lark asked Hunter as they slowly made their way up the mountain, watching Shelby at the head, acting like it was nothing at all to scale this huge rock.

"What? Hike? Yeah, she's done it almost every week for the entire year that I've known her." Hunter said absentmindedly, matching Lark's pace as they continued.

"No, this, playing matchmaker. How many people has she set you up with?" Lark could see Hunter's cheeks turn red, and he turned his gaze to the mountainside instead of the pretty girl beside him.

"Don't be too mad at Shell; she did it as a favor. I do like your books, and I wanted to meet you. The old Hunter wouldn't have tried to talk to you a year ago. I've learned the hard way that if you don't take chances, things slip through your fingers. It's funny, Lark, how things have changed for me in the course of a year."

"I don't mean to pry, but what exactly happened to you? What changed you so drastically? I mean, it must have been something pretty epic." Hunter finally turned his gaze back to the girl and nodded.

"My friend, Drew, and I work for the Finch Hollow Hospital. We are medical examiners and double as private investigators for the town Chairman. There was a rash of teen suicides, and Drew and I... Well, we stumbled onto some pretty heavy stuff."

"I couldn't help but notice the scars on your hands. Did that happen last year, too?" Again, Hunter nodded and looked up at his friend, who had vanished over a rather large slope in the mountainside.

"She's beating us big time," Hunter said with a crooked smile. "How much you want to bet? She took her tether off and wandered up without her safety gear. She's horrible for that."

Little did Hunter know how true his words were. She had, in fact, taken off her ropes, but that was because she had found the mouth of a cave right over the slope of the mountain. She knew that others had climbed this mountain, had taken the same route she had, and not one of them had told her about this cave. She couldn't pass up the opportunity to investigate. The cabin would be there later, and this was the perfect place to rest for a little while.

Pulling a water bottle from her pack, she sat at the mouth of the cave for a little while. Drinking her water slowly. Ever since the Factory burned down, the towns' water had begun to taste... funny. They told the townspeople they had to add special chemicals to it to prevent radiation from leaking into the drinking water. Shelby wasn't sure she believed them, so she always drank bottled water.

She had only been sitting there momentarily when she thought she heard a noise further into the cave. She was no stranger to the possible dangers that a cave could hold. Sudden drops, wild animals, or poisonous fauna, but she couldn't help but become curious about where the sound was coming from and what was causing it. Slipping the water back into her pack, she got to her feet and ventured into the darkness. She stopped about five feet in; the sound had gotten quite a bit louder, and she knew for sure now that what she was hearing wasn't some wild animal or waterfall. What she was hearing sounded like music. It sounded like old-school saloon music. She could almost hear the people inside talking and clinking glasses.

Her confusion deepened when she looked down and noticed something small and shiny. Grabbing her pack from her shoulder again, she removed a small flashlight and shone it onto the cave floor.

"Hey, what ya doing back there?" Shelby could hear her friends enter the mouth of the cave. Hunter had yelled back to her as he helped Lark up over the slope.

"You'll never believe this, guys!" Shelby said as she bent over and picked up what looked like a ruby necklace lying on the ground. "It sounds like there's a party going on down here."

"A what?" Lark began, but that was all the three could say before the mountain began to shake and jump.

"What the hell is going on!!" Hunter yelled as he grabbed onto Lark's arm to help keep her steady.

"I don't know," Shelby yelled back. She wanted to keep searching the cave but knew that if this were an earthquake, the chances of a cave-in were rather high; turning around to meet back up with her friends, Shelby could take only two steps before she heard the cracking under her feet. The grip on her flashlight and the necklace tightened as she looked down and realized the cave floor was opening up.

"Shelby, get back here! The quakes are getting worse!" Lark yelled. She tried to venture into the darkness to get her friend, but Hunter stopped her.

"Trust me, Lark; you do not want to do that. It's suicide, and I've seen enough of that in my lifetime to hold me over until the next." Lark was going to push past the man, but she could see the pleading in his eyes and knew he was right.

Shelby was afraid to move. She didn't know what to do. Inching her way closer and closer to the mouth of the cave, she could see the silhouettes of her friends as the mountain continued to move and dance about like one of those motion-activated toys that sang stupid songs. Hunter took a few steps towards her and reached out his hand.

"Come on, Shell; you can do this." She also reached out to her friend, dropping the flashlight at her feet. It rolled around and fell between the cracks in the stone. The light vanished into the darkness, and so did Shelby as she let out a scream of terror when the cave floor opened up and swallowed her whole.

"Nooooooo!" Lark screamed as she grabbed Hunter's hand. It was good that she did because he almost slipped into the nothing as well. Falling back against Hunter, the two of them fell by the base of the cave. The quakes had stopped, and the two got to their feet.

"Oh my God, Hunter, what do we do?" Hunter wrapped his arms around the girl, who had begun to sob uncontrollably.

"We need to calm down and think rationally. We need to find the bottom of the mountain and call for help. My cell is in the glove compartment of Drew's car. Hell, his is probably there, too. He was never too good at keeping up with it. It might take us longer than usual without Shelby helping, but we can do it." Pulling away from Hunter, Lark nodded in approval, and they began their hike back down the slope and onto the face of the mountain once again.

CHAPTER FOUR

Shelby fell into the nothing. She had braced for impact, but the feeling of floating had begun to take over her whole body. She had shut her eyes when she had first fell, but now had gathered enough courage to open them. The music she had heard was all around her. She could smell the cigarette smoke; she could hear the saloon doors swing open and shut as the patrons entered for their pints of ale; she could hear the shuffling of cards at the poker tables and the laughter of loose women picking their Johns for the evening.

Still, all she could see was the black, inky nothing around her. Her skin had begun to go cold. Her arms and legs were all tingly from swimming in the thick abyss that was the nothing. Once again, Shelby looked down at her hand and realized she still had the necklace. Something inside told her to slip it around her neck, and she did so without hesitation.

She immediately began to fall, fast and hard; she hit the bottom with a loud thud. Her head hit something flat and solid.

"Hey, boys, looks like this one may have had a little too much to drink. What do ya'll think?" The sound of the man's voice caused Shelby to lift her head and look all around the room she was now in. Sure enough, she was in an old-school saloon.

"Where am I?" She muttered as she looked around the bar.

"The Twisted Star, Ma'am. Nice of you to drop in." The voice was right beside her, and she looked over at where it had come from. The others who had taken a slight interest in the new woman had already wandered off, which had just left her with this man, a shot of whiskey in his hand, and the barkeep who was minding his own business drying the beer mugs on the other side of the long wooden desk.

"When are we?" Shelby asked as she began to rub her head. The man let out a bold laugh and took down his shot of whiskey. Slamming the shot glass back onto the table, he motioned for the bartender.

"Quinton, give me another." The bartender walked over and refreshed the man's drink. Shelby had begun to look around the room. The dusty old saloon looked like it had come straight out of an old western. All the men in the place were wearing old chaps, grimy leather cowboy hats, and spurred boots, and no one looked like they had taken a shower in weeks. She began to look down at what she was wearing and was shocked to see that she had on a red brothel dress, one that matched the necklace she had slipped over her head right before reentry.

"Best I can figure, it's the 1920s; I got stuck here too, Ma'am. Some stupid cosmic joke, best I can figure."

"What do you mean? Is this some sort of time rift or something? I mean, more than likely, I'm at the bottom of the cave, unconscious, and you're all just figments of my imagination." This perked the man's ear up, and he looked at the girl with renewed interest.

"A cave, you say?" Shelby nodded and grabbed at her neck to ensure the necklace was still there. It was. "The names Samuel Jersey. Son of Buck. I'm sure you've heard of me." This time, it was Shelby's turn to laugh.

"That's impossible. You would have to be in your eighties; you don't look a day over twenty-five."

"That's what happened here, Miss... I didn't catch your name."

"Shelby, my name is Shelby Willton."

"Well, I surely don't know if we are in purgatory or what, but I've been reliving the same day over and over for what seems like forever. The first thing you have to know is that I was, in fact, in my seventies and sitting at the table in the Guild's office. Stardock had told me about the resurgence, and BOOM! I'm back at the Twisted Star, having drinks with my dad's old friends. I'm the same age as he was when he left for Coral Bay that fall day when all this stuff began to happen." Shelby tilted her head to one side and smiled her dimpled smile at the man.

"Samuel, there's no way I'm going to believe that. The stories of the sisters were greatly exaggerated. Even if they were true stories, which I highly doubt, they are long past gone. Why would anyone want to do this to you? Or to me? No, I'm hallucinating; I have to be. You know, there are types of moss in caves that make people see things that aren't there." Samuel covered his face with his hand and let out a huge sigh.

"This is what I'm talking about right here. I told the guild that we needed to reach out, that keeping this resurgence a secret could put all of the human race in danger... again... and that keeping all ya'll safe was the whole purpose of the guild."

"The guild, you mean the guild of magics. The fake, made-up, highly imaginary guild? The one that has their very own halfling fairy on their side? If fairies were real, and trust me, in all my 23 years on this planet, have I ever seen a fairy? Stardock would have eaten you all alive. They are killers."

Samuel couldn't believe what he was hearing. This poor girl was clearly in denial, and he rested his head on the bar in utter surrender.

"Can you at least tell me what year it is? I would love to know how long I've been drinking at this bar."

"Twenty-twenty-one." Again, the information made the man sit up and stare at her, confused.

"I've missed it! The resurgence! Someone must have stopped it, but who?" Shelby shrugged her shoulders and grabbed for the necklace once again.

"All I know is that my friends and I were going to climb Beast Mountain. We found the cave, and I came across this necklace." Shelby pulled the necklace from her dress. Samuel's eyes lit up even brighter.

"Beast Mountain, you say... I may have a way for us both to get out of here."

CHAPTER FIVE

Hunter had to keep a hand on the back of Lark's shoulder to keep her from falling down the cliff. She had been a much better climber on the way up, but her panic and fear for what had happened to Shelby had caused her to trimmer. She had managed to keep her calm enough to stop crying, but Hunter could tell that it was just a disguise to make him feel better as well.

Even though, from the outside, Hunter seemed to be taking things a lot better than his friend, on the inside, he was freaking out, too. He knew that telling her would have done neither of them any good.

They had made it about halfway when Hunter thought a little conversation might take her mind away from the emergency.

"Lark, I wouldn't worry so much about Shelby. She is an accomplished climber. I bet she's making her way out of the cave right now... Looking down at us and laughing or something."

"Yeah, that's something she would do alright," Lark muttered as she looked down at the base of the mountain. She knew it would be a little while before they could get to the cars... Before they could call for help. He knew that Hunter was only trying to help. In his own way, on another day, for another reason, Lark would have found it endearing and couldn't help but smile over at him in reassurance.

Hunter thought that Lark might have been, at that very moment, the most beautiful girl he had ever seen. Her hair was covered in soot, and she had dirt on her cheek, but he could see the beauty in her soul, and that made him like her even more than before.

"I know it may sound weird, but I've been through much worse than this not too long ago, either."

"Really?" Lark asked; she thought it might be another way for him to distract her, but she took the opportunity to let him whisk her away to another world... At least until they could get to the bottom of this mountain.

"For real. You really want to know how I got these scars?" Lark nodded, so Hunter continued. "Well, last year, to be fair, it hasn't quite been a year now, but it sure does feel like another lifetime has passed. I guess those things do when you go through something like this. Anyway, I'm getting off topic."

"Go ahead; I want to hear your story," Lark said. He could tell that the girl was feeling a little more secure, so he allowed himself to let go of her shoulder. Now that he had more control over what he was doing, they both were able to climb a little faster.

"As I told you earlier, we had a rash of teen suicides all over Finch Hollow. It was unlike anything my friend Drew and I had ever seen. The things I saw over a week or so were crazy, to say the least. The Police didn't even believe half of what we told them, even though two of them were there for the grand finally."

"Sounds like a wild ride," Lark said as she placed her foot on a large rock protruding from the mountain's north side.

"You have no idea. It all started to get weird when we took in the body of one Darla Snead. She was a local kid with no enemies, but she was dead at the base of the church tower, and no one had seen anything that had happened. Lark, this girl woke up on the slab. She was dead, but she wasn't." Lark snorted, laughed, and looked at the man again as they continued their trek.

"That is impossible." She said, rolling her eyes.

"Funny, coming from someone who writes fiction for a living," Hunter said, rolling his eyes back at her.

"Fair enough, but I know reality from illusion, and someone had to be messing with you guys."

"I'm sure that's what Drew had initially thought, too. My first thought was, "Oh shit, a zombie!" I was also convinced that she was going to eat us... In hindsight, I wasn't too far from the truth. We learned about this death curse and how these two villages, standing around Finch Hollow like a million years ago, waged war on each other. Anyway, the last five families, after being cursed for five generations, enchanted the living children to kill themselves, but they didn't count on Darla's mom being an honest-to-god witch."

"A witch?" Lark scoffed. "You can't be serious."

"As a heart attack." The monotone in the man's voice made Lark realize that he was being serious. The girl shut her mouth and continued to listen to Hunter's story.

"Drew and I found out that she had used this spell book to put this sort of life-sucking symbols on three of Darla's friends. When we tried to stop her from hurting the other kids to keep her own alive, she attacked me with a knife. I had to grab the blade with my bare hands. There was a struggle; she ended up killing herself." They had almost reached the bottom of the mountain. But Lark wanted to hear the end of the story, no matter how ridiculous it may sound.

“So, did you two manage to save the kids?” She asked as their feet touched the solid ground for the second time that day.

“In a manner of speaking. Maybe, after all of this is over. After we get Shelby home, I can tell you about a few more scars I have. I’ve got a bunch of odd stories about that week.”

CHAPTER SIX

"What did you have in mind?" Shelby asked as she looked around the bar. Tucking the necklace back between her cleavage, she looked at the man. He had been looking around the place like he had been expecting company.

"Every day around this time, two men enter the bar looking for Buck. They all think I'm him. Sometimes I go along with it; sometimes I don't. I know how both scenarios play out, but now that you're here, we may have a third option." Samuel put his arm around Shelby as he heard the saloon doors open and the familiar voice of someone coming up behind them. Turning around on the barstools, the two looked at the men who had entered the bar.

The first was a fat little man with three chins and a face for radio; the second was tall and thin, dressed to the nines. He wore a top hat and had a little briefcase in one hand. Shelby couldn't help but look at the tall man. Where had she seen him before? His face was so familiar.

"Mr. Jersey?" The fat man asked as he walked over to Samuel. Nodding, Samuel held out his hand.

"Who's asking?" Samuel said, even though he knew, good and well, who was, in fact, asking.

"The name is Carter, Carter Jones, and I work with the Woodsmith in the little township of Coral Bay. I'm sure you're aware of the little infestation that town is experiencing, and we thought that your little gang of rag-tag men would like to get in on the ground floor before the fairy revelation hits and the train makes its last stop." The fat man shook Sam's hand and stepped back, allowing the tall man to take over the conversation.

"It took you long enough to get here." He said, looking over at the girl. Samuel opened his mouth to say something, but shut it quickly. How did he know this blond woman? She had only just entered the bar. After all this time, Samuel thought this place was a mere simulation, and all the players except himself were on repeat, for lack of a better word.

"Excuse me?" Shelby asked. "Do I know you?" The thin man smiled and took the woman's hand.

"Not formally. I did get the chance to visit your small town a while back. Quite charming. Coral Bay hasn't changed much in the last hundred years." Samuel grabbed Shelby's hand and pulled it away from the man's grasp. This action only made the man smile wider. It almost looked unnatural and started to creep the two of them out. "Well, now that the gang's all here, you'll have to return to your old time. I can't believe how easy it is to manipulate you, people. How easy it is to weave my agenda with your little guilds." The man stepped back and allowed the saloon doors to open independently.

Keeping a firm grip on Shelby's hand, Sam pushed past the two men and stepped out of the saloon. As soon as they did, the bar vanished into thin air, leaving them in the middle of nowhere. All around, all Shelby could see was a dustbowl. Almost as if they were in the middle of the desert.

"What do we do now?" She asked the man, who still had his hand laced with hers.

"My father was on the way to see the Wood Smith. His name was Arkadi. He told me that they had to go through this tiny town on the other side of the mountain. He could see the castle perched on the top, so they thought they didn't have much further to go. He thought he could stop at his favorite watering hole in these parts called the Twisted Star. That's where he met my mother. She had given up all hope of him ever returning, but when he did, he was war-torn on the way back to the boy's and had adopted a little girl named Molly." The two of them had begun to walk away from where the old tavern stood to the west of the sun. Shelby thought that the man had a plan. Hopefully, he knew what he was doing because she certainly did not.

"I'm all for story hour, but what does that have to do with returning home?"

"Well, Buck loved to talk about his old lady. Her name was Pearl, Pearl White. Had me at the ripe old age of twenty. Last I heard, she lived a long time... Like longer than anyone had the right to. He told me that she had followed him to the base of the mountain. That she didn't want him to go. He told me a long time ago that there was a cave at the base of the mountain. If you did things right and had the Mother's Heart, you could open the door inside the cave. You brought the key." Shelby looked around the old dusty nothing. She couldn't make out more than five feet in front of her.

"I don't see a mountain." Shelby began, but the man put his free hand in the air.

"Never you mind that. I know where I'm going. This is the most far I've gotten before the fat man shoots me in the back. I have a feeling, though, that isn't going to be the case today." The two of them continued to walk, and mere minutes later, they were standing at the base of the mountain. Sure enough, there was a large cave mouth right in front of where they stood.

On the left side of the mouth was a divot, the same size as the red stone on Shelby's necklace.

"Quick, give me your necklace," Sam said, holding out his hand. Shelby was hesitant but took it off and handed it to him anyway. After all, the man looked like he knew what he was doing. Reaching the divot, Sam was about to put the stone in like a key, but stopped when he heard Shelby from behind him.

"Wait," She began. "What happens if we go back through the portal... or whatever, and you're eighty again... What if this isn't the way home?"

"Ma'am, I can't stay here forever, and seventy-three is a long time to be alive. You need to go home, and so do I." Shelby nodded and allowed the man to continue what he was doing. Putting the stone into the divot, the mountain, once again, shook and quaked, making the whole ground under their feet crack. Dust and dry dirt flew up around them. Within moments, a cream-white door appeared right inside the cave opening. Snatching the stone from the divot, Sam pulled Shelby inside with him. He reached for the door handle, but she stopped him one last time.

"Before we go, where are we exactly?" Sam smiled and looked over at her. Opening the white door, he pulled her through.

"They used to call this place Shadows End."

CHAPTER SEVEN

Victor Zanborn sat in his office behind a black rod iron desk. His room was decorated with diverse types of bluebells and morning glories. He never went anywhere without a few in his pocket. Victor was no stranger to the dangers of the fairies and what exactly a bite from one of those buggers could do to human flesh.

Sipping on a mug of tea, which held just a dash of witch hazel, he looked down at the papers placed there just a few hours ago. His team had long disbursed to their own homes, but Victor had bigger fish to fry than sitting alone in his two-story townhouse at the edge of town.

Picking up the top paper, he looked at the photo attached.

"Lark Henson." He muttered to himself. "Why would you get tangled up with the likes of Hunter Williams, and better yet... Who would have compelled your friend to invite him?"

"I think I can answer that question." A voice echoed through the big office. Putting the paper down, Victor looked over to the door. Standing in the doorway was Stardock. He had an extremely tough time coming much further into the room; everything inside of it was meant to ward off his type.

"Well, don't be shy, Doc, give it to me straight." Victor didn't care for the fairies, but this one had been immensely helpful, and for some reason, the man had grown a soft spot for the creature.

"I've been following the girls. I know that you didn't ask me to, but there is something about that Shelby woman... She may have deeper roots than we all thought at first." Victor nodded and motioned for the little man to continue. "Well, the night that Lark came to town, I noticed another Fairy. At first, I thought it was just your average run-of-the-mill monster, but upon closer investigation, it wasn't. Sir, I am certain that Lark and Shelby met with the Fairy King Deaththorne." At the sound of that name, Victor sat upright in his chair and put a hand in his front pocket.

"So, the resurgence has gained momentum, has it not? I thought we would have more time. The men stopped the first wave; we should have had more time." Stardock nodded, leaning a shoulder against the door frame.

"That's not all. I know that he tried to enter the house, but I had the witch put a blocking spell on all the doors and windows. Deaththorne couldn't enter, but I know the King has other ways to glamour humans." Again, Victor nodded and sat back in his chair.

"Wonderful work, Doc, keep it up. Lark, she found the door, right? She has to get to the gunslinger before the new moon." Stardock looked down at his feet and began to shuffle them.

"About that..." He began, and Victor got to his feet this time, walking over to the little man. Stardock had always been a little scared of him, even though Victor had never given the halfling a single reason to be. He hovered over most of the people in the guild at a whopping six foot seven. He was a thick man with broad shoulders and large, ogre-like hands. He rarely smiled, but when he did, it always looked unnatural and scary.

Victor had a mop of grey hair on top of his rather large head that he never bothered to comb. His brow was always furrowed as though he were on the edge of a fit or angered by something. Stardock couldn't help but think it was because of his past and what had happened to him when he was younger. You see, the death of fairy magic didn't kill all magic. Some of it always had a way of creeping in through the cracks, causing chaos and tipping the scales of normalcy.

It was a normal spring day in the town of Crimson Ridge, where the Zanborn family lived for the better part of a decade. Victor had two daughters, Rose and Allison. His wife, Lesly, took the girls to the park. Victor had to stay home and work. He had just started his internship at the Guild and worked as a teller at the local bank to make ends meet. At first glance, you would have thought this was just another typical family, but you would be wrong.

That night, when his girls returned, things weren't right. Victor could tell right away that something had happened, but all of them refused to open up and say a word. By the next morning, his girls were all dead. No one, not even the medical examiner, could give the man a cause of death, and every night, he would be visited by the souls of his three loves. This went on for months until he forced himself to move. If he hadn't, he would have surely gone mad.

This was the moment that Victor promised himself that he would find out what happened to his family and devote all his time to the guild so he could find every way possible to stop evil from creeping into the cracks again.

"What do you mean by that, Doc? She was supposed to get the slinger out of the paradox and write about it."

"I... She did write... something, but I don't know what it was." Stardock shifted his feet once more, and Victor softened his stare. He knew scaring the little man would be of little help to anyone. He only did what he thought was best, and Victor commended his efforts.

"Well, what exactly happened, Doc? We need to know."

"The night that Deaththorne visited the women, something stirred Lark from her slumber; I could see her through the bushes in the backyard, she wrote for a long time. I couldn't tell what she was writing, sir, because the King had perched himself beside the big tree. I followed them to the mountain; Shelby, she found the cave, not Lark; Shelby fell into the paradox, not Lark." Victor tilted his head to the side; he didn't know what to make of the situation. He had always thought that Lark was the one they were counting on to get the slinger, to save the day... Lark was their hero, but now Victor wasn't so sure.

"Maybe you should watch the girls for a little longer... See what Lark wrote, and please, Doc, find out all you can about Shelby Willton."

CHAPTER EIGHT

The police had come and gone, and there was no sign of Shelby or the cave. Even after Lark and Hunter had wholeheartedly insisted there had been. Now, the two of them sat on the hood of the yellow beater and tried to collect their thoughts.

"Well, what do we do now, Hunter?" Lark asked as she wrapped her arms around herself. The sun was setting, and the temperature had begun to drop.

"I honestly don't know; I don't feel like I can leave here... Not just yet. Something is telling me to stay put."

"Maybe we should call your friend, Drew? You said he was good at solving things like this." Hunter looked over at the shivering woman and hopped off the car hood; walking around to the back, he popped the trunk and pulled out an old wool blanket.

"Yeah, maybe we should." He said, walking around to the front of the car and wrapping the blanket over the slender girl's shoulders. "It's scratchy, but it's warm. Drew always keeps one in the trunk just in case."

"In case of what?" Lark asked as she pulled the wool blanket tighter. He was right; it itched her skin, but it knocked the chill off almost immediately.

"In case a victim at a crime scene needs it." Hunter pulled his phone from his front pocket and made a second call that night.

"Hello?" Drew said he answered on the second ring, which was customary when he was at the apartment. If he had called Drew's cell phone, he would have found it under the passenger seat in the yellow hooptie, which was also customary.

"Hey, it's Hunter; we may have a situation here."

"What kind of situation?" Drew asked as he popped the top off the first beer of the night. It had been almost too quiet in Finch Hollow Ever since Mark and his band of cult members had been eliminated or arrested, and Andrew was itching for a good mystery.

Almost daily, he missed Matthew and William, and he hated the idea of never knowing who he actually heard on the other side of the door the night they took Hannah home. She had chosen to move to another town and start college. Hunter felt obligated to help her pay for it since she had been orphaned. He all but adopted the girl because that was the kind of guy Hunter was.

"Not quite a Darla, but we have a missing person," Hunter said on the other side of the phone.

"Well, I don't have a whole lot going on here. I could take a few days off and try to help out if you want." Drew said as he took a sip of his cold beer. It was his favorite part of the night.

"That would be great. See you tomorrow?" Hunter asked,

"See you tomorrow." Andrew agreed as he hung up the phone, turning his attention again to his suds.

Slipping his phone back into his pocket, Hunter looked at Lark, who was fixated on the sunset behind the hill.

"If this were any other moment, I would be in heaven right now, looking at this breathtaking sunset, wrapped in warmth in good company." Hunter couldn't help but smile. He understood what the woman meant. He couldn't think of another person he would have rather been with in that moment.

At first, they thought it was just their imagination, the way that the ground began to move around them. Almost as if it were breathing. But after a few moments, there was no denying it was happening again. Lark jumped out of the car and backed away from it.

"What the Hell is going on?" She asked as she looked over at Hunter in confusion.

"I don't know..." He said, but his eyes widened as a plain white door emerged from the base of the mountain, one with a simple brass handle. "Oh no, not again." He muttered as he began to back away, inching towards his car. He grabbed Lark's hand and tried to take her with him, but she was far too intrigued.

"Again?" She asked as she took a step closer to the door.

"Please, Lark, you don't know what's on the other side of that thing." The rumbling stopped, and the door began to inch its way open. Lark's eyes were as big as saucers, her mouth open in childlike awe.

"Hey, a little help here!" A familiar voice called from the blackness.

"Shelby?" Lark squeaked and ran to the door, prying it open. Within seconds, Shelby and Samuel were standing on the other side of the door, and it slammed shut behind them, but it didn't vanish.

"Oh, man, that took a minute. There are a ton of doors in there." Shelby said with a grin. Samuel smiled at her, then looked over at Lark. His expression changed from happy to concern.

“Oh, hell no. I know you!” Sam said as he began to back away from Lark.

“What do you mean?” She said as she took a step towards the man.

“This is Samuel Jersey, the son of Buck Jersey... Or so he says. We were stuck in some time rift down in the cave. I know how unbelievable that sounds, but that’s the best way to describe it.” Hunter looked over at Shelby and the man, and then down at his hands.

“Actually, Shell, it’s not the craziest thing I’ve ever heard.” Hunter walked over to the man, looking him up and down. He was dressed as if he had just come from a Western. He had two silver revolvers tucked into holsters on either side of his belt, and his hands were inching towards them, almost as if the man thought Lark was going to do something horrible. “What do you think you’re going to do there, buddy?” Hunter asked, extending his hand for the man to shake. He was hoping to distract him from Lark’s presence, but it didn’t work. Samuel took another step back, and the bewildered look on Lark’s face only got more intense.

“Look, Samuel, I don’t know who you are. My name is Lark, Lark Henson.” Samuel laughed heartily and again took another step away from the girl.

“You don’t fool me; you’re the perfect likeness to your mother. Where are you keeping them?”

“Keeping who?” Lark asked. She thought she was confused before, but now she had fallen right into the feeling of utter insanity. "I think you have me confused with someone else." Again, the man laughed and began to shake his head.

"You can try to confuse me, but I know what kind of person you are. You look small and harmless, but when that man took my sister away, he gave her powers... Those powers stayed in the family tree. If she had them, so do you."

"Look, Samuel, Lark here was adopted, so that might be why she doesn't know what you're talking about, and quite frankly, I don't know either. I've known her for as long as I can remember, and she's never taken anyone or done anything nefarious." Upon hearing Shelby's words, Samuel began softening his stare, and his hands lowered by his sides. Hunter had walked over and stood in front of the girl. He couldn't have handled the thought of her being shot and injured... Or worse.

"Oh, my apologies, ma'am. I thought you knew who your parents were."

"Did you know my parents? Could you tell me about them? I was adopted when I was little and don't really remember." Taking off his hat, the man took a few steps closer to Lark. He placed the hat over his chest like he was going to deliver some unwelcome news.

"Believe it or not, your mother was my adopted sister, Molly Jersey. She fell in love with an awfully bad man named Murdock." A look of clarity crossed Shelby's face.

"That man, the tall one at the saloon, that was him, wasn't it?" Samuel nodded. "But how could that be? He came to town a few years ago; he bought up the old bakery; shit got really weird around here for a while. He can't be that old, Samuel. He just can't."

"That's where you're wrong, Ms. Shelby; he's much older and much meaner than any of you know. I know in your time, this would sound wild, but hear me out before you write me off as an old coot."

"You're not old; what are you? Like thirty?" Hunter said as he took Lark's hand. She let him and thought how much he wanted to comfort and protect her was endearing. No one had ever done that for her before. Samuel looked down at his hands and realized that the boy was right and let out a little gasp.

"Well, hot damn, the rift let me keep my youth. How about that?"

"Apparently, when he went in there, he was in his eighties. If he is who he says he is, then yes, he would be in his eighties, but I mean, no one has heard from Samuel Jersey for decades. Even when there was documented evidence that he was real, the stories had to have been greatly exaggerated."

"Ma'am, why do you keep saying if I am who I say I am? Why would I lie about my name? You saw what was down there." Shelby still had a challenging time gathering what had happened. She had always wanted to believe in magic, but now that she had seen it with her very eyes, her common sense wouldn't allow her to understand. "Look, Murdock wasn't... isn't a man. He's pure evil.

Not all of them are like he is, and no one knows what made him into the monster he is today, but Molly enchanted him. I don't know if he loved her beauty or innocence more. I use the term love loosely because I'm not entirely sure that thing could love anyone. He stole her away in the middle of the night, the night that he had gathered his last story."

"Story? He was a writer?" Lark asked; her attention had swayed into utter fascination. She had never heard about her birth parents. Her foster family wouldn't tell her a single thing about them, only that they weren't fit to raise her. She often daydreamed that her birth parents would return and take her away from her boring old life. Even as a child, she knew she was destined for great adventures; when they didn't come, she created them inside of notebooks and now, inside of her little blue laptop.

"Heavens, no," Samuel said with a little grin. He was a collector of horrors–unleashing monsters and collecting the souls within the pages of his journals. We had thought that the man had run off and killed Molly, of that we were very certain, but that wasn't what happened. Her fate was far worse than death."

"What happened to your sister?" Hunter asked as he squeezed Lark's hand a little tighter. He could tell she was caught up in the moment, and they had just met the man. How much of this could have been true, and how much could have been made up? Hunter knew from personal experience how weird and supernatural this place could be; no one knew with more clarity that the unknown could sneak up behind you in your backyard and bite you right where you stood.

"He married her, and he gifted her with the power of manifestation on their wedding night. He essentially gave her the power to write things into existence."

"Why would he do that?" Lark asked. She could feel the chill through the wool blanket and stepped closer to Hunter. His warmth helped the icy chill that had begun to slide down her back.

"Well, my dear, so he could feed off her stories, take the souls of the people she crushed with her quill, and have her body as well. She had three daughters: the first in 1942, Melinda Monroe; the middle child, and possibly the worst of them all, born in 1950, Merry Belle Monroe; and then you in 1998, Mercy Monroe. I was beginning to look into your history when I was... wait a minute, did you?" Hunter looked over at Lark with a furrowed brow; she could see the concern in his eyes.

"I remember that book, Lark; it was one of your firsts. Wasn't it called the Star of Shadow's Peak?" Lark let out a little laugh; the chill on her back had now become an ice burg.

"That's impossible. I can't write things into existence. No one can; that's just ridiculous." Sam stepped closer to the girl, putting his hat back on his head.

"There's only one way to know for sure."

"And how is that?" Hunter asked.

"Let's look at all her literary work; let's see if we can match it up with things that have happened around here."

CHAPTER NINE

"What the hell are we doing here, Deaththorne?" Misty had been walking with the little man since the sun had set a few hours ago. She thought getting a cab would have been a better, more efficient way to get to the next town, but Thorne figured it would raise too many red flags.

"We have to get the items; you've promised to bring back my Queen, and that is what we are setting out to do right now." The woods they had been walking through had become quite thick, and the brush knocked Misty in the face, making her extremely agitated.

"Why tonight? Why right now?" She muttered under her breath. It was the coldest summer night, and the breeze blew around them.

"Because Misty, tonight is the night that we get to spill the blood of the damned, and it has to be in the field of the Starshallow flowers. We should be coming to them at any moment." Misty could feel the excitement rushing through the fairy's body; Heat was coming off of him so intently that steam had begun to rise from his grey skin.

Walking out of the dense forest and into the field of purple flowers, the moon had shone down on them like a spotlight. A smile crossed the little monster's face as he stopped.

"Why did you stop?" Misty asked as she made her way into the field.

"I can't go any further; none of us can; that's why we needed you and your ruthlessness to bring back what we need. The field is treated with poison for us fairies, bluebells, and morning glories. If I set one foot inside there, I would surely turn to dust." Reaching into the pouch Deaththorn had been carrying behind him, he pulled out a small stone blade. Handing it to Misty, the creature slumped back into the darkness of the wood. "You need to use this; you need to corrupt the tree with the blood of the damned; that way, you can break a branch off of it to make your wand. It is imperative that you do not touch the flowers, pick them, or smell them until you have done so, and for the love of all things magic, never pick the blue ones or the ones tainted with blood." With that, the fairy vanished into the night, leaving the girl standing at the base of the field, wandering where the blood of the damned might be found.

It wasn't long into her trek that the girl saw a tree in the middle of the field, and under it, bathed in the moonlight, stood two women. It wasn't hard for the girl to see that the two of them were clearly related. Both were beautiful in their own way, dressed all in white, Roman-style gowns, kneeling under the umbrella of the weeping willow. Misty didn't hesitate or waver in her task; she knew what she had to do, and she would do it no matter the cost. She wanted the little demons off her back, but the girl hungered for power even more, and she would stop at nothing to get it.

The first woman was a little taller than the second, with long, curly locks of red hair that ran down her back, like the vines of the Red Mandevilla. Her skin was milky white, and the moon caused it to shimmer like Selenite. Misty thought she had never seen such beauty in all of her life.

The second woman was a little shorter, with her red hair tied up in a bun and small wavy wisps cascading down her cheeks like a waterfall of blood. She also had milky white skin, but what caught Misty's eye was the woman's large, pouty red lips. The Roman gown accentuated her curves. Her heart had started to pound inside her chest. She had never felt nervous like this before about killing another human, and then the thought hit her like a ton of bricks. Maybe these women weren't human. Hell, the fairies weren't human; why did she automatically think that they would be too?

Slouching down in the tall grass, she began to inch closer to the women. As she approached, she could hear the song they were repeating as they laid their hands on the tree. It was a catchy little tune that could get caught in your head if you weren't too careful, like an earworm eating away at your sanity.

"She whispered from the breeze, she whispered from the trees, branches reaching to the earth, head towards the sun, her power inside her leaves, all witches return as one." Misty had paid this chant no mind as she ventured ever closer to the twins.

"You only have to take one of us, you know." The taller girl said as she pulled a strange fruit from a low-hanging branch. "You know that eating from the mother tree will give you the knowledge of a thousand years." Misty knew now that there was no point in hiding from the women. She had figured it would have done her little good to have tried from the start anyway.

"He sent you, didn't he?" The second witch asked. They were both looking over at her now. Their eyes were large, wide-set, and emerald green. If Misty hadn't known better, she would have thought their eyes had been replaced with crystals. The moonlight bounced off them like a disco ball. Misty thought she could stare at them forever.

"No offense to either one of you. I'm just doing what I have to do to get the little ankle biters off of my back." The two of them tilted their head to the side in unison. Their smiles were beautiful but full of darkness. Misty felt the hair on the back of her neck stand up. She had never met anyone as evil as herself before. It was refreshing and terrifying all at the same time.

Running towards the smaller woman, knife in tow, Misty let out a battle cry, but it was short-lived because, with just a simple wave of her hand, the witch threw her back away using nothing more than the breeze from the frosty night air.

"Do you honestly think you're any match for the Monroe sisters?" The shorter woman walked over to Misty, who had fallen onto her back. The soft grass had helped her out a little, but the oxygen had still been knocked out of her. "I am Melinda, and my sister over there is Marry Belle; we have come to reclaim what is ours and retrieve our little sister before he corrupts her evil." Misty took her chance and swung the knife at Melinda. Unsuspecting, she instinctively put her hand over her face to protect it, and the blade cut through the skin on her arm like butter.

Thick, hot, red blood streamed from the beautiful woman's arm, and she cried in surprise and anger. Getting to her feet, Misty ran her hand across the witch's wound and stumbled towards the tree.

"You don't know what you are doing, little one." Mary Belle said as she walked to her sister's side. Melinda was now sitting on the ground, and everywhere the blood fell, a new blue flower began to bloom.

Smearing the blood across the tree, Misty grabbed the first branch she could find and broke it without a second thought. When she turned around, the two sisters had vanished into the night. Where the hell did they go? She thought to herself as she wandered into the field and snatched a few flowers without thinking. None of them that she could see had any of the witches' blood on them, but she wouldn't have been able to tell the difference between the ones there from before and those that bloomed when Melinda's blood hit the soft earth. She thought that Deaththorne would have to figure that one out on his own.

CHAPTER TEN

Samuel had insisted on walking back to the guild; he had no use for the trio of kids he had met back at the mountain. In fact, he made it more than clear that Lark would begin to change if they dug too far into her past and urged them to keep their search focused on her storytelling abilities and nothing more. Shelby thought the man might have known more than he was letting on, but she didn't want to pressure him. After all, he did give them quite a bit to go on. Maybe he wasn't as weird as she had first thought.

The idea of the things that she had read as a child being real fascinated her, but like Lark, she knew in her heart that this type of stuff wasn't real. What self-respecting adult goes around ranting and raving about witches and fairies? Well... Believing in them anyway.

Going back to Shelby's house, the three of them had a late dinner, and Shelby vanished into her room after taking a shower, leaving Hunter and Lark alone. Before too long, the two of them had ventured onto the little blue laptop, and Hunter had begun to skim through some of her older published novels. He had read most of them on more than one occasion, but it had never occurred to him to do an internet search on the things that happened in a so-called fiction book.

"You've only really been writing for a little over a year, right?" Hunter asked as he scrolled through one of Lark's oldest books.

"Yeah, I submitted a novel to several publishing agencies, and this one was the first to respond. They offered me a salary way above what someone as new as I was deserved. How could I turn that away?" Hunter nodded as he continued to read.

"You know, I might be one of the most open-minded people you're going to meet when it comes to weird stuff happening. I've seen a door like the one Sam and Shell walked through tonight... A year ago, to be exact." Lark's eyes lit up when she heard about the door.

"What is it?" Lark asked. She almost couldn't believe what she had seen tonight. She would have laughed it away if she hadn't seen it all with her own eyes.

"I've never been through the door myself, but two of my friends went through and... Well, they haven't returned. They might never come back, but they thought that what they were doing was for an honorable reason... Something that could save a lot of people. There!" Hunter said, pointing to the computer screen.

"What?" Lark said as she tilted over the leaning man's shoulder.

"There, you wrote this scene, one where an evil temptress entrances three kids from a local town to bring back the soul of an innocent one that held three lives, one for each of the kids." Lark looked over at Hunter and rolled her eyes.

"Yeah, nerd, it's called exaggerative writing. It keeps people on their toes. What about it?"

"I don't want to be a bummer here, but that's what happened to Darla. You wrote about her in this book, and it came true. By chance, is there an evil villain at the end of the book that tries to destroy the town through lies and trickery? Was there a weird ass cult?" Lark tilted her head and squinted her eyes.

"You've read this one already, haven't you?" Closing the laptop, Hunter looked over at her and shook his head.

"This one slipped by me, but I might have been able to piece this together last year when it happened in Finch Hollow and Eagles Nest. They both can share credit for that hot mess."

"What does that mean?" Lark said, even though she knew good and well what it meant. Samuel had said that she was writing evils into the world, or at the very least, writing about their coming.

"I don't know for sure what the next course of action is, but just to be safe, let's not write anymore for the time being, okay?" Lark looked at Hunter oddly and tapped her finger on the kitchen table. "What? What is it, Lark?"

"Well..." She began, I may have written something already." Opening the laptop up once again, Lark opened the icon labeled Willow Tree. The three chapters popped up on the screen, and Hunter began to read. It didn't take him long to get through it because he always enjoyed what the woman wrote, but he became concerned during the last chapter.

"I really liked the beginning of the story," Hunter began, but when he turned to face her, she had a thousand-mile stare that pierced his very soul. He could look into those green eyes for hours.

"What part did you like the best?" she asked as she stepped closer. Hunter didn't know what to do. Should he step back or take a chance and step toward the beautiful woman?

"I like the main characters; they have good chemistry," He said with a grin. Lark took another step closer and placed a tiny hand on the man's face. Her stare never left his, not for a second.

"I think they do, too." Taking the final steps toward Hunter, they would have been nose to nose if it weren't for the height difference. Getting on her tippy toes, she put her other hand on Hunter's other cheek, and he gave in, leaning over and kissing the girl for the first time in the little rustic kitchen right on the edge of town in Coral Bay. At that moment, everything in the world melted away; his skin tingled, and his spine felt like electricity. He had never kissed like that. Never in his life...

After a few seconds, though, his senses returned to him as he remembered the last chapter.

"Lark, chapter three." But that was all he could get out before the two of them were plunged into darkness.

"What's going on?" Lark said as she wrapped herself around Hunter's arm. He pulled her in close, and they both made their way to the kitchen drawers. Hunter knew the precursors to a flank attack. He had found out all too well at the hotel.

Opening the top drawer, he used his free hand to rummage around, and to his relief, he pulled out a rather large knife.

"What are you going to do with that?" Lark said as she looked at the large blade. She could see the reflection of her face on the shiny metal, which triggered her memory. "Oh my god!" She exclaimed, "Chapter three!" He couldn't tell if the girl had been in some trance for the last few moments, but Hunter would have liked to hope she remembered the kiss. In any case, they had to get to the other end of the house before what Lark had written came true.

"Why would you write something like that?" Hunter whispered as they inched their way down the hall toward Shelby's room. So far, everything had been silent, but that would soon change.

"I didn't know... I didn't... Do you think that kiss? The one"

"I remember," Hunter said with a smile.

"Well, do you think we did because we wanted to or because I wrote it that way?" Hunter sighed and stopped long enough to look into Lark's green eyes again. He had never witnessed such beauty in all his life.

"I don't know about tonight, but I've always wanted to kiss you. Even before you wrote what you did. You fascinate me."

"Even now, even though I'm a freak?" Hunter smiled as he continued to walk towards Shelby's door, Lark behind him, holding on for dear life to his free arm.

"Even more so now." He whispered back to her. Suddenly, they heard the window on the other side of the door smash to bits and Shelby screaming from her room. Hunter ran up and knocked the door open with a single kick, releasing the horrors on the other side.

"Get off of her!" Hunter yelled as he held the knife in front of his face reactively. The fairy smiled, looking over at Hunter. They had never seen anything quite so horrifying. It's flabby, grey skin held loosely upon its slight frame. Its smile reached from ear to pointy ear, and it had one large, clawed hand around Shelby's neck.

"What are you going to do, warrior? You could attack, but you know I would rip the princess's throat out far before you could stop me." The monster's smile grew, almost encompassing the entire bottom of its face. Hunter could make out sharp, jagged teeth behind those thin lips. Those, he thought, were the teeth of a man-eater.

"What do you want?" Hunter bellowed but thought better than to take any quick steps toward his friend.

"Please," Shelby whimpered, "Help me." Lark's head was spinning as she tried with all her might to remember everything she had written the night before; her sleep deprivation didn't help at all. In her book, the troll slipped inside the princess's bedroom, killing her as she slept. Stealing away a priceless ruby necklace. It wanted to please the Troll King and Queen with it. The story she had written wasn't exactly how she had envisioned it on the laptop. This led her to believe one thing... She wasn't making things happen. She was telling the future.

"I need the red stone. The king has abandoned us for a human nonetheless; without this grand gesture, he will forget us completely." The thing tightened its grip on Shelby's neck and lifted her into an upright position on the bed. Her hair fell around her neck, a cascade of curls flowing like breathtaking diamonds down the front of her gown, framing her pained face. Putting her hands on the monster's, she tried to pull free to no avail.

Scanning the room, Lark saw what the thing was looking for and snatched it from a half-open drawer.

"Looking for this, short, fat, and ugly?" She said as she made her way back out of the door and into the hallway. Letting out a scream of anger, the monster released Shelby, who fell back onto the bed with a gasp. Lunging towards the beast, Hunter took a swing with the knife but missed, and the fairy, with the force of three men, grabbed Hunter by the assaulting arm and threw him across the room and onto the floor beside the bed. With a groan, Hunter rolled over. He could hear the thing's feet padding away in pursuit of Lark. Shelby rolled over and looked down at the man. She had red marks on her neck; they may bruise, but the thing hadn't done any permanent damage.

"What are you waiting for?" She said as she reached down and helped him to his feet. "Go save your girlfriend." Hunter had always respected how Shell bounced back from things, but this was unimaginably impressive for a single day. Turning to the open door, he couldn't see more than three feet into the darkened hallway. He still had the knife, and he hoped his aim would be better this time.

Lark had made it into the Living room before the thing caught up with her. She was fast, but the fairy was quicker and the stronger apex predator. Running towards the front door, she reached out to open it, but the little troll grabbed her by the ankles, and she was down on the floor within seconds. A snarly laugh escaped the thing's lips as it rolled her over onto her back and pinned her hands over her head. Sitting upon her stomach, it craned its neck unnaturally and smelled her hair. Grinning, it opened its mouth, exposing sharp yellow teeth. Lark couldn't help but whimper and turn her head to the side. Closing her eyes, she waited for the thing to bite her face off.

"Get your hands off of her!" Hunter yelled, causing the fairy to ease up on its grip. Opening one eye, Lark could tell it was distracted and took the time to struggle, freeing one hand from its grasp... The hand with the necklace. It had been wrapped around her knuckles as she had run through the house, and now she was going to use them as brass knuckles. Swinging for the fences, Lark punched the little booger in the face with all of her might. Letting out a howl of pain, it turned to face the girl once again, and once again, a look of horror washed over her face. Opening its mouth, the monster lunged down to bite her on the neck. With seconds to spare, Hunter threw the fairy off of Lark. Flying a few feet across the room, it landed on the end table on its back. The two of them could hear the crack of breaking bones, and when it got to its feet, they could see why. One of its wings had broken almost off.

Limping like a drunken sailor, it began to walk towards them.

"Give me the red stone."

"What's your name? What are you?" Lark asked as she got to her feet and stood behind Hunter, who had once again pointed the knife out in front of him like a sword.

"I am Corrowin; we are all Corrowin. We are the fairies. Give me the red stone." Waving the knife in front of the fairy, Hunter took another step back. It had begun to bleed on the carpet, and Hunter could tell that the blood wasn't like ours. It was black and inky and had started to bubble. The smell of burning sulfur began to fill the living room. Horrible and thick like rotten eggs. At that moment, Hunter knew he couldn't use the knife and looked at Lark.

"I don't know what to do." He whispered. But that was the last thing he got to say before Shelby emerged from the hallway, a piece of rod iron in her hand. Letting out a battle cry, the woman rushed the little beast and drove the staff through the back of the nightmare's head.

As soon as she thought that she had done what she came in there to do, she ran towards her two friends and pushed them out of the front door. Looking through the window from the outside, the three of them watched in horror and disbelief as Corrowin began to shake violently and then fall to the floor. His little fat body began to fill up, almost like a balloon on a helium machine.

"What's happening?" Hunter asked. What he was witnessing in Shelby's living room was unreal. The fairy's little wings tried to fly, but only made it flip over onto its belly, then onto its back. One of its little beady eyes had popped out of its head. The swelling continued until his body began to crack and pus. Everywhere the monster bled, the floor started to smoke; it got so smoky inside that they could barely see what had happened when they heard a large pop! Black ooze covered the window. They didn't need to see the carnage to know that Corrowin had been blown up.

"How did you know what to do?" Lark asked, looking over at Shelby.

"You wouldn't let me finish the story last night. I didn't know that thing was a fairy until it all but told you. Once I heard that, I remembered their weakness: Rod iron, blue bells, and Morning glories. I just happened to have some of that metal in my crafting room. I was going to make a fence for the garden. Figured it was on the way to the living room, couldn't hurt to take a chance."

"And stabbing anything in the head would pretty much guarantee a kill," Hunter said, looking over at Shell.

"Well, yeah, that too."

CHAPTER ELEVEN

"No, no, no, no!!!!!" She said as she began to pace around thc room. She had her hands behind her back, looking directly at the floor.

"That's what I'm telling you, Ann. It's not all on Lark, that girl... Shelby, there's something about her." Samuel looked over at the witch and shook his head as she continued to pace the floor.

"I tried to tell Victor as well," Stardock said. He had sat down on the other side of the room instinctively. He knew that Samuel wouldn't hurt him, but gunslingers were notorious for outbursts of rage, and he didn't want to be in the middle of the room when it happened.

Ann Key Bearings was, for lack of a better word, the guild's resident witch, even though she was no witch at all. The first and possibly the only creature of her kind. She had the body of a normal person, broad shoulders, dark raven hair with just one thick streak of blond running down the right side of her head; she had the pointy ears of a fairy and two marble blue eyes that tended to glow when they hit the sun. Her skin was pale, with a hint of pink to it. If she stayed outside too long, it almost looked like she had put glitter on. She was both breathtaking and deadly when she needed to be. She could take on the persona of any supernatural element, which made her a jack of all trades. Unkillable, at least as far as the guild could tell.

Ann didn't like being called the witch, but she let it slide, for lack of a better word. Hopefully, one day, she would find out who she really was; until then, she was stuck in the cabin on the top of the mountain with the rest of the weirdos. They had moved there after the resurgence. They all knew that the second wave was coming, and now they were right in the thick of things. Unaware that it had even started.

"How could this have happened?" Ann muttered and then stopped pacing. Looking over at the halfling, she tilted her head with a look of revelation. "What did you do, Stardock? All those years ago, what did you do?" Samuel looked over at the little man and leaned closer toward him.

"What do you mean, Ann? He seemed to have been just as shocked as I was when he laid eyes on her, hell, even more so to hear him tell it." Ann once again focused on the gunslinger.

"Oh, he may have been surprised, but I don't think he doesn't have any answers, Sam." Motioning for Stardock to come closer, the little man couldn't help but hesitate for a moment. He knew that she was right, and he knew what he had done eighty years earlier was wrong, but those were different times, in a different world, and he was human then! He felt things so differently than he did now. Even today, though, he probably would have made the same choice. He had never killed another human, and he prided himself on that. It was, after all, in his nature to do so. "You knew what it said in the book of the mother tree about what was to happen to all of us, to every supernatural element, if the Southpaw lineage continued to flourish. We could all be in some deep shit now, Doc. You have to tell me what happened." Looking down at the ground, the halfling took a deep breath and took a few steps closer to his friends.

"I thought I was doing the right thing. Before you get upset, just know I thought I was doing the right thing."

"Hell, Doc, I always figured your heart was too big for your little body. I ain't never seen you do anything malicious, but how could you think that keeping the Southpaw bloodline alive was doing the right thing?" Samuel asked. He had leaned back in his chair and put an elbow on the bar beside him. The first thing he did when he returned to the guild was make himself a decent whiskey sour. It wasn't like he hadn't had enough at the Twisted Star, but the bartender wasn't great at making much; Sam had given up trying to order anything other than shots after a while.

"Well, you see, Buck and Pearl had just had you,1933, and I was kind of in the background, what with Molly turning nineteen, getting ready to move to another city and go to school. I knew I had time on my hands, and this would have been the perfect time to check in on the Mad Nobleman. We thought of him as a non-threat at the time. The beast had taken his sanity, and the neighboring village was happy keeping him under lock and key."

"I've heard all of this before, Stardock," Ann said as she crossed the room and sat down in the chair next to Sam. "Get to the part where there is a possibility that we have been living in a world with a Southpaw. One where this ticking time bomb is mere miles away."

"I... I heard crying from the cell. Ann, Henry had a baby in his hands, talking gibberish as usual. But how did he get the baby? I really couldn't tell you that. What I know is that if I had told Buck, he would have killed the poor little thing or, worse, asked me to do it. It took some convincing, but Henry allowed me to take the baby. I didn't even know if it was Henry's; you have to believe me. Either way, I wanted to be safe, so I took the little thing to the nunnery. I made Sister Agnus promise me that the little angel would never leave the grounds. I guess she didn't live up to her promise." The room was silent momentarily, but then Sam spoke up, lifting his glass towards the little halfling.

"Here's to you, little Doc, for always keeping us on our toes."

"Well, what do we do now?" Stardock asked, looking over at Ann; she had begun to rub her temples. He could tell she was stressed out and probably needed a good walk in the sun to get her mood back in the correct order. She was a sun creature and required to be in the light for a set amount of time each day to maintain her powers. Without it, she tended to grow irritated and weakened. In fact, one time, when she had to go out into the night, she put on a long-hooded cloak. When Stardock asked why she had chosen to do so, she responded with the words. 'I tend to get moon burn.'

"I think the best course of action is to wait until morning and bring the whole lot of them here to the guild. I couldn't care less about the boy, but Mercy won't leave his side at this point, for that I am certain."

"I can contact Victor if you want him inside the loop. Ya know, I don't like doing things without his approval." Sam said as he got to his feet. Ann nodded and pointed towards the door.

"I wouldn't be too surprised, Stardock, if you get grounded to the cabin while the three of them are here... Seeing as how you love to babysit and all."

CHAPTER TWELVE

Murdock rarely liked to be the center of his own story, but it was the way it had to be from time to time. He had left the mirror world when the fairy revelation happened, crossing the doors to other mirror worlds and creating chaos and violence wherever his feet touched down. Murdock was a creature of simple means; he only craved the darkness inside, which ate away at humanity as a whole. Some would say 'evil' or 'the devil,' but Murdock knew better. This darkness didn't just creep inside like a spider and its web, not this thing inside of everyone, even the best of us; this darkness was part of the spider.

He had let thirteen years pass. Thirteen was his favorite number. He always asked for thirteen stories, which he usually got. Now and again, though, he would get an extra one as a treat. Some people had more darkness in them than others. Scouring the town for the best person to approach, he happened upon a cobbler and his beautiful wife, Dell. Standing by the open window, he listened in on their conversation. Murdock had no quims about eavesdropping or extortion if it got him what he wanted.

"Theo, what are we going to do?" Dell asked as she paced the floor of the little cottage.

"I am doing the best that I can, love. I have tried to get more business, but times are rough; we will make it through, though." Theo responded as he continued to work on a pair of children's shoes. Dell sat by the front door and put her head in her hands. It was bad enough that she had married a man with such few means, but everything that she had dreamed of seemed to be slipping away.

The nobility that had lived just on the other side of the mountain had given this town its flourishing economy. Still, after their brutal death and the destruction of the town, only a handful of families were able to rebuild.

"It's hard enough to know that I will never be able to give you a child, but I refuse to sit here and starve to death with you as well, Theo Zanborn!" Murdock thought this would be the perfect time to approach the family. He had much business to attend to and would love some good reading material.

"Maybe I can be of some assistance," Murdock said, tipping his top hat at Dell through the open window. The girl smiled, but Theo seemed unamused at the fancy man's intro.

"Whatever you're selling, we aren't buying." Theo began, but Murdock put a slender finger in the air and vanished around the corner, only to enter through the front door.

"The name is Monroe, Murdock Monroe, and I am a peddler of happiness. I couldn't help but overhear that you need money. If you want, I could make that happen... All the money you could ever need could be yours."

"Theo!" Dell said, putting her hands over her mouth. The thought of never having to struggle again was heavenly. This time, Theo stopped his work to look at the man, scowling.

"I can care for my family just fine without your help." Murdock's smile began to widen. He loved a good fight. He could smell the pride ooze off the man like a cheap cologne.

"Well then, maybe that's the ticket I'm looking to buy then... A family? Would you and your wife like a child?" Again, Dell couldn't help but let out a little squeak. How could Theo pass up the thought of a baby? They had tried so many times and failed each time. He had always said it would happen if it were meant to, but Dell knew better.

"Mr... Monroe, is it?" Theo said with a little irritation in his voice, "I'm going to have to ask you to leave. You're giving my wife thoughts of things you cannot deliver, and I cannot have that in my house." Holding his briefcase in front of him, Murdock nodded and left the cabin. He was nothing if not in this for the long game. The longer he waited, the better the darkness tasted.

Every night, he would return to the house, and every night, he would be turned away. It had begun to be a game to the tall man... Until the last night, when Murdock returned to the house after dusk to find Dell on the front stoop, standing under the lantern.

"Why, Dell, what are you doing out here this beautiful evening?" Murdock asked as he approached the woman. He could tell she had been crying, and he didn't care much about it. Human weakness sickened him, but he did his best to feign concern. "My dear, what on earth is the matter?" Dell looked over at the man, and he could see the pleading in her eyes.

"Mr. Monroe, I want nothing more than to have Theo's baby. We have been trying, but I don't think I ever will." Murdock looked around, but Theo was nowhere to be seen. He also thought this to be weird because Theo tended to be quite protective of his wife. Murdock doubted that he would have allowed her to be out here alone.

"My dear, where exactly is your husband?" Dell shrugged her shoulders and sat down upon the stoop.

“He left a few hours ago; the best I can figure is that he’s drunk at the saloon.” Murdock knew now was the time to seal the deal. He didn’t need Theo’s agreement to ruin his lineage, which made Murdock incredibly happy. Opening the case in front of him, the man pulled out a piece of paper and a red pen. Kneeling in front of the broken woman, he handed them to her. “What is this?” She asked as she looked down at the paper.

“I don’t normally do these sorts of deals, but I do need gifts for three very important people; you see, someone wrote about them a few towns over, and I’ve come to collect the package they come in.” Dell seemed confused but continued to listen to what the man had to say. “You will have your child, you will get to hold him, and you will be content for a price.” The man’s smile began to widen, and that always made Dell’s skin crawl a little. He had never been anything but a gentleman, but she knew that there was something darker behind that kind face.

“What’s the price?” She asked with a stutter.

“Nothing that concerns you, not in your lifetime, but I will be needing three Zanborn souls. One for each of my gifts.” Dell thought hard about the price and knew that it was selfish, but agreed and signed the paper in front of her. She would stop at nothing to have a baby and a boy to boot? Theo would be over the moon about it. He didn’t have to know about the deal; he didn’t have to know about anything. If it were meant to be, then it would happen.

Now that the first of thirteen had begun, he began to make his way to the next town over, to Crimson Ridge. He just loved saying that name, and he loved the way that the trees bloomed in the spring, with all the red foliage. She was right where the story had told him she would be, inside the coffee shop, nose in a book.

Molly Jersey had been accepted to Crimson Ridge College for applied technologies. It was a real culture shock moving from just one town to the next, almost like walking through a time loop. Murdock didn't understand why he felt nervous; he'd never felt that way, and he didn't like it at all. He had heard about the girl, the small one that survived the fairy revelation with little more than a gnarly scar on her shoulder to show for it.

Molly had no friends save for a little man named Stardock, who was never too far away; well, tonight was the exception, tonight the little weird one had other things to do. Approaching the window, he took another look at the pretty girl and walked into the coffee shop, where there was electricity and heat that ran through the whole building. He spared no time walking over to the booth where Molly sat. She didn't even notice the man until he was sitting on the other side of the booth.

"Can I help you?" She asked as she put her book down and took a sip of her hot coffee.

"I certainly hope you can." He said with a smooth tone. Molly had never met the man before, but there was something familiar to him, almost comforting, and if Molly had realized that it was the evil inside of him she felt so attached to her might have run that very night.

Putting his briefcase on the table, Murdock opened it up and pulled out a journal. "I'm not completely sure, but I believe that this is yours." Sliding the journal across the table, Molly picked it up and looked it over.

"I don't think so." She began but opened the book and began to read, drinking in its words like a fine wine. "I, um, I..." her words began to wander off as she continued to read. The stories were loud inside her head. Murdock could see the journal begin to change her, the way the woman who wrote it explained in graphic detail; Molly's brown hair began to grow and turn red, her brown eyes taking on an emerald hue, and her skin losing most of its pigmentation. Yes, this woman would be his bride; she would bear him three gifts, and he would give her the power of the journal. She was almost pure perfection.

As they drifted off into the night, no one knew what had taken place, and no one would know until it was time... When the witches take on their father, the second wave of magic and the passing of the torch.

CHAPTER THIRTEEN

The three of them had wandered back into the house just long enough to grab a piece of rod iron from Shelby's crafting room. Each of them was now carrying a weapon; Shelby slipped on a pair of her sneakers and her purse, and Lark got her laptop and wallet. All the while, Hunter just stood at the base of the living room, right outside the front door, in glorified awe. He never thought for a second that he would have gotten the chance to see a fairy, let alone talk to one.

"You got the keys?" Shelby yelled back to Hunter as she tied her shoes. He felt around in his pocket,

"Yeah, let's hurry up, girls; we don't know how many of these things are out here." Lark emerged from the kitchen and quickly made her way out the front door to Hunter's side. She slipped her free hand into his, and they patiently waited for Shelby. It only took a few moments before the two of them could make out the headlights of a rather large dark vehicle in the distance. At first, the two of them didn't think anything of it, but when it pulled to a halt behind the yellow beater, they took notice.

"Hello?" Hunter asked, squinting his eyes to try to make out the figures inside of the black government-issued SUV. Suddenly, the back door opened, and out stepped Andrew, wearing the same trench coat and fedora Hunter remembered all too well. "Drew!" Hunter exclaimed with a smile. "What are you doing here this late? I thought you were coming tomorrow."

"When you told me that we had a situation, I dropped all the stuff I was doing and came right over. Looks like it was a good thing that I did. What the hell happened in there?" Andrew pointed to the window that was covered in gross black goop. The glass had begun to crack and sizzle, and the smell had wafted out onto the front lawn like a thick custard.

"It's a long story... You remember when I said it wasn't a Darla thing?" Andrew nodded and walked over to the front yard, wrinkling up his nose as he got closer. "Well, I might have been too quick to judge. We found our friend. Drew, though, there was another door." Drew's eyes widened as he took a few more steps toward his friend.

"Like the door from last year? The one that Matt and Will went through?" Hunter shook his head and let go of Lark's hand for a moment.

"No, not exactly. Drew, this was a new door." Shelby emerged through the front door, shutting it behind her, and looked over at the new person on the front lawn.

"Who is this?" She asked as she shifted the piece of rod iron from one hand to the other.

"Shell, this is Andrew Bower. Drew, this is Shelby and Lark. He's come to help us figure out what the hell is going on." Hunter and Drew looked over as the front window rolled down, and a familiar face popped out.

"I've been looking through some of the classified documents you had a bit of interest in, Drew, and you won't believe what I found out."

"Thanks, Keen, but first, I think these three have had enough for one night. Let's get a few rooms and crash for a few hours." Drew said as he motioned for the three of them to get into the SUV. Hunter threw the keys to the old beater at his friend.

"Thanks for letting me borrow your car. It's been an experience." Drew nodded at his friend as he walked over to the car to get inside.

"Hey, let's go to the hotel on Dodson," Shelby said as she began to get into the car.

"Why?" Drew asked.

"Because they have rod iron bars on all the windows. Probably the safest place we could go right now."

The five of them made their way to the hotel and got two rooms for the night. The girls in one and the guys in the other. It only took a few minutes for Lark to fall into a heavy sleep. The trauma of the day's excitement had taken its toll on the girl. What she wasn't expecting was to wake up in a black abyss of nothing.

All she could see was the black void. No ceiling, no floor, and no way out. She could see herself as she looked down, almost as if she were illuminated, but other than that,... black.

"Hello?" She called out, but the sound of her own voice echoed all around her and rattled around in her head like a bad radio song on a car trip you can't unhear. She thought in the distance, she could hear the soft cries of a baby, and the thought of something so innocent in a place like this gave the girl instant depression. She could feel the cold dark, nothing against her skin, and the unimagined silence in the void was almost as unbearable as the hello still dangling in the air like a balloon.

"Mercy." She could hear a woman's voice; it was quiet... Almost like a whisper in the air, but she could hear it, and it was there, giving her hope that someone was in there with her, that maybe they knew the way out.

"Who's there?" She whispered back into the nothing. She could hear the drip of water and feel moisture on her skin. Everything felt so surreal, and she knew that she had to be dreaming, but how could a dream be this lifelike?

"We have been searching for you; we need you. We are your sisters." Scrambling to her feet, Lark began to walk through the nothing. It felt like wading through quicksand, and the longer she tried to move, the more she began to struggle, and her breathing became labored.

"What... What do you want?" Lark gasped as she continued to walk towards what? She had no idea. "I only hear one of you."

"Stay with us, Mercy; we need you." At this point, the girl could barely breathe, and she began to scratch and grab at her throat. "Let go, Mercy, let go and be with us." Falling onto all four, Lark continued to crawl towards the nothing when she saw a tear in the void, a small sliver of light, and then a long, thin arm, which reached through the throes of time and took her wrist.

As she was drawn closer to the light, she could hear the woman who called herself sister growing agitated. "Do not let him pull you through the gate; he's evil, he will come for your friends... You'll be damned!" That was the last thing she heard before the arm pulled her almost lifeless body through the tear, and she fell face-first back onto the hotel bed with a thud.

Letting out a gasp of fresh air, Lark rolled off the bed and onto the floor. Shelby emerged from the bathroom with a towel on her head. The sun had risen, and Lark had guessed she had been in the dark nothing for the majority of the night.

"Good, you're awake; I was gonna get something to eat. You hungry?" The thought of food turned the poor girl's stomach as she rolled over onto her side and threw up beside the bed. Black goo emerged from her mouth, bubbling onto the floor and then sizzling into nothingness as the sun from the overhead window hit it. "Oh my God, Lark!" Shelby exclaimed and came running to the girl's side. "What happened?"

"Get the guys," Lark said with a gasp. "I think we have another really big problem."

CHAPTER FOURTEEN

"Raaahhhh!" Deaththorne screamed as he threw the flowers across the room at Misty. She covered her face, but a few of them landed in her hair, making her look like a bridesmaid. "Why did you not listen to my words, child?" Approaching Misty, who was sitting on her cot in the cabin, Deaththrone pointed a little crooked finger at the girl who wasn't at all frightened of the fairy's advances. "I should eat you for this, giving me those tainted flowers." Smirking, Misty leaned towards the little man and reached behind her back. There, she had hidden her favorite little garden claw, and she wasn't afraid to run it through someone's skull. She had done it once before and wouldn't hesitate to do it to the fairy king if he made any attempt at harming her.

"You can certainly try, but your little buddies weren't very successful, and I doubt you would be either." Deaththorne leaned back a little and retreated to the other side of the room, covering his face with a long, grey hand.

"We have to go back; we have to do it right, Misty." The sound of her name crossing his lips was like fingernails on a chalkboard to her, and she cringed a little when he spoke. "The blood you spilled was from the eldest witch; you should have killed her. The life force fell from her wound and sprouted moon-shadow flowers. They are useless to us. We must go back." Misty sighed and looked around the room. All she ever wanted was peace and quiet. Now, she would have to go back to the field and snag some old weed that this eccentric thing thinks would bring back his wife.

From what she had heard before, Mara Lafea had died during the revelation. Those stories had been told around the campfire for generations now. Misty had never believed them, but now she wasn't so sure.

"Can you tell me, once again, how exactly we are going to get your queen back?" Misty said, propping her elbows upon her knees and pulling a small bag out from under the bed. Inside were oranges and dried meat that she had made herself a few weeks back. Deer meat was her favorite, and she had become quite good at hunting.

Taking his hand off of his face, Deaththorne walked over to the girl as she offered him some of the meat. He took it eagerly and ate a few pieces before talking to her.

"There's a door; it will appear once we have the Mother's Heart. The littlest witch has it now, and she will help us once she realizes what her sisters are up to."

"Why do we even need the flowers and the stick?" Misty asked, peeling the orange. The smell of citrus filled the room with a light, springtime vibe that Misty loved. Deaththorne, on the other hand, held his nose and scooted away from the girl. The smell made him gag. Too sweet, too fresh.

"Starshallow flowers are the only thing that will draw her from the door, and she must have the wand. It is the center of all her power." Deaththorn took another bite of the meat as his eyes drifted away from the girl and her horrible fruit. Misty could tell, in the monster's own way, he cared for the queen, and it confused her. She thought that the fairies only had hate, hunger, and rage in their little black hearts. Maybe it was the lack of power and the dwindling numbers of his kind that gave his face such a sour look.

"How do you know she will be there?" Misty asked, taking another bite of her lunch.

"She will, it is written in the old texts; the second resurgence will be that of the fairies, and the last remaining Southpaw child will lead them against all who had worked against them. It's odd, really, though, that the Southpaws would help us... After we tried to kill them all." Misty tilted her head as she finished the orange and turned to the deer meat. She always saved the best for last.

"You were just doing what you thought was right at the time. The revelation told you that if the sisters died, there would be no rapture for your kind. We wouldn't need Southpaw's help now if you all had succeeded in your attempts." Deaththorne shot the girl an evil stare and snarled.

"Watch your tongue, girl; you have no idea what you are talking about. Do not insinuate that we were weaklings or fools. The Southpaw bloodline runs thick, and the sisters were more powerful than you would ever know... Not to mention the boy, Samuel. His love for the little blond one reached no limits. The plan was doomed to fail."

"Well, let's hope that this one hasn't booed up yet," Misty said with a snort. Again, the fairy eyed her with daggers, but this only made Misty snort louder. She loved to irritate the wee man. He knew that he needed her, at least for the time being, and without the Queen, he had little to no real power.

"Tonight, we will go and get the flowers again. I will do the best that I can to look them over before we retreat back to the cabin. I thought I could trust you before, but now I know better." Deaththorne finished his meat before retreating into the back room for his day's slumber.

"Yeah, well, that was your first mistake, little monster, to think you could trust me," Misty said as she took the last of her meat and slid the bag back under the cot.

CHAPTER FIFTEEN

Keen had pulled out his government-issued palm computer and typed a few things into it while the others sat around the table at the local diner eating breakfast, all except for Lark, who still didn't feel much like eating. She had gotten a little color back into her face, but everyone could tell that she wasn't at her best.

"Are you sure you won't eat anything?" Shelby asked as she tried to offer the girl a piece of dry toast.

"No, thank you. I just can't... Not right now." Shelby nodded. Hunter, who was sitting on the other side of Lark, put a hand on her leg and looked over at her. She smiled and put her hand on top of his. She didn't know why, but the simple act of being close to the man was both comforting and reassuring. Maybe it was because she had written it; perhaps she had created these emotions between the two of them. She really hoped that it wasn't the case because she could feel herself truly falling in love with the boy she had barely known for two days, and that was something that had never ever happened to Lark.

"Ah, here we go. This was what I was going to tell you about before." Keen said as he put the palm computer down on the table and pointed to a little blurb on the screen. He had highlighted the most important pieces in yellow.

"The Guilds of Magics, President of chapter 151, Victor Zanborn, relocates team to Eagles Nest." Drew read as the others leaned in closer.

"Guilds of Magics? What exactly is that?" Hunter asked as he turned his attention to Agent Keen.

"I'm not one hundred percent sure; it's over my pay grade, but I have heard a little about this group... and about this Zanborn fellow."

"Well, spill it," Drew said as he slid the palm computer back to his friend. Keen nodded and slipped the device into his breast pocket.

"Okay, well, Victor was this normal type of guy that lived over in Crimson Ridge a while back, and his family... well, his wife and two daughters, they all died, and no one could figure out how it happened."

"I bet we would have figured it out," Hunter said as he took a bite of his eggs and continued to listen to the story.

"Maybe, but this was before your time," Keen said. Drew leaned back and scratched his head, wiggling the little hat that was perched on top. Shelby couldn't help but smile at the man. He had an endearing way about him that she quite enjoyed.

"I vaguely remember this. I was new to the job, I think, but it did sound suspicious. No marks on the bodies, no toxins, medical conditions, gases... Nothing, and the only living person in the house that morning was the father, Victor. Didn't he move away or something?" Drew looked back at Keen, who was sipping his coffee. He nodded and put the cup back down on the table.

"Yes, he basically vanished. Well, that's what the guild wanted you to think. He actually went to work for the Guilds of Magics; they were at the edge of town in the south district of Shadows End."

"Wait a minute, you mean to tell me that the old factory was where they were? So close to me, and I didn't even know it? You don't think they were watching me, do you?" Even as the words were coming out of her mouth, Lark knew that she sounded a little paranoid.

"I wouldn't doubt it. It is called the Guilds of Magics for a reason, and I couldn't really think of anything more magic than a trio of witches. Hell,

Drew and I had to face one witch, and she put up a gnarly fight; if there were three of her, I doubt we would have made it out of the apartment alive." Lark squeezed Hunter's hand and smiled at him.

"Well, if I am a witch, who remains to be seen, and I do have two sisters, like Sam said, and who have not made a real-life effort to find me, I contest now that I will be a good witch. Even if I have some evil force inside of me."

"What else do you know?" Drew said, drawing everyone's attention back to the large agent who had begun to eat his plate of fruit.

"Well, according to this article, they moved last year, and you won't believe where."Hunter and Andrew looked at each other as the realization hit them both.

"No," Hunter began.

"You've got to be kidding me." Drew followed.

"What? What am I missing?" Shelby said, taking another bite of her bacon. Drew looked over at the blond girl and shook his head.

"The cabin up on Eagles Nest, the one with all the cult members and the Beast."

"The Beast?" Lark asked.

"It's a bit of a story, but I think you would be more inclined to believe it now that you've seen some things," Hunter said as he took a sip of his own coffee.

"You two will have plenty of time to fill them in after breakfast," Keen replied as he continued to eat his fruit.

"Why is that?" Drew asked.

"Because last night, while you were sleeping, I called in a few favors, and you're all invited to stay there until we can sort all of this out."

CHAPTER SIXTEEN

Melinda and Merry Belle were the first two gifts to be granted to Murdock, even though he was barely ever there. Each one had their own story, but this one is the story of Mary Belle and how she became known as the most wicked witch in all of the mirror kingdom. Even at a noticeably early age, Merry Belle was the most beautiful girl in all of Shadow's End, so lovely, in fact, that when she walked into the room, time would come to a halt. It is a falsehood that Murdock gave the sisters powers; no, that would be too easy, you see. All of the girls had their own unique set of gifts, and Merry Belle's was that of persuasion; she could convince anyone, male, female, alive, or dead, to do her bidding and grant her every wish.

She was tall and slender, with perfectly set emerald eyes. She never cut her long red hair because, for some reason, she felt that was where the root of her powers came from. As much as she was her father, Murdock, she was also the beautiful Merry Belle, a woman with emotions and a real need for companionship.

Merry Belle had only turned sixteen when she had happened upon a boy, not just any boy, but the boy of her dreams. He was dark and strong, and the sound of his laughter could ring through the clouds like the song of Adonis. She knew she could have the boy with a mere look, but didn't want to get him with magic; it would have been far too easy, and she loved the thrill of the hunt. She got that from her father, she supposed, but was it really that bad of a quality?

In those days, in Shadows End, 1966, to be exact, there was little to no crime, and the children were sent out into the streets to play until the streetlights would turn on, and this day was no different. She had watched the boy with his friends, and now that the dusk was upon them, they had dispersed into the night to venture to their own homes. Her love was no exception.

"Hello," Merry Belle said as she caught up with the boy, matching strides with his stride. The sound of her voice was enough to startle him. He had thought to be by himself, but smiled and nodded at the girl.

"You on your way home too?" He asked, and she nodded, even though her house was on the other side of town. That was of no consequence, though, because her sister and her mother cared truly little about Marry-belle's whereabouts. They knew she could take care of herself.

"My name is Merry, what's yours?" The boy slowed his gait a little, trying extremely hard not to make eye contact with the beautiful girl talking to him. Was this a joke? He thought. Who put her up to this?

"It's Rigney, Rigney Lancaster. I think I've seen you around. You don't go to school with the rest of us, do you?" Merry shook her head and slipped her hand into his.

"No, mother wanted us to be homeschooled, my sister and I. I fear I may have told you a little lie earlier. I live in the opposite direction, but I wanted to talk to you alone."

"I know," Rigney replied, "I kind of wanted you to talk to me." That was the beginning of a wonderful relationship. You see, she didn't have to use her magic to find love, and everything was going swimmingly. How did this make Mary Belle the most vicious witch in the history of Shadows End? Just wait for it...

In the fall of 1968, Rigney and Merry Belle wandered into the Monroe home to have a little tryst. This was something they would often do when Melinda and Molly ventured into town for supplies; on this day, though, Melinda had stayed home much to the surprise of Merry belle, and when I say surprise, I mean when she had left her lover and ventured from her room, Melinda had slipped in using the power she had recently grew into, and in that moment, when Merry returned to see, Rigney with her sister the rage inside of her was too much to bear.

"How could you!" Merry screamed, throwing anything and everything she could at the two of them. Melinda ran from the room to escape Merry's wrath.

"I thought... I thought..." That was all that the boy could get out before Merry Belle lifted him off of the bed with another power she had gained, a power that took the strength of her rage to fill. She lifted the boy off of the bed with the power of her mind and threw him through the bay window. He fell two stories down and landed on the concrete fountain below, cracking his skull at the base of the fountain and filling the clear water with red swirls of thick brain matter. She still could not contain her anger, her anger for her lover and for everyone in town.

To Merry Belle, the whole town was laughing at her, pointing at the used girl; somehow, to Merry, they all knew her shame that Rigney was a cheater. What Merry didn't know, though, was that Melinda had gained the power of glamour and could make people see what she wanted them to. Rigney had thought the girl in the room was Merry Belle.

Merry rampaged through the small town, systematically getting people to turn on each other. Shootings, stabbings, burnings... You name it, and it happened. She stood in the middle of town for a while and watched her handiwork until the guilds of magic put a stop to her. The Monroe family had to flee from Shadows End, and on that day, a scorned witch killed 151 people.

CHAPTER SEVENTEEN

"Oh my God, would you look at the sheer size of that gate!" Shelby was already star-struck by the notion of getting to walk the grounds of the old cabin. Keen pulled up to the gate and punched in a few numbers. Drew could hear the buttons' beeps and feel dread build in his chest. He couldn't shake the feeling of doom that painted the whole mountain. His friends had almost died inside the cabin; how could he be going back up there... Better yet, how could the people living there now be okay with staying there?

"You ready?" Keen asked as the gate doors opened, and he slowly drove through them and up the winding road.

"I'm not sure," Drew muttered as he looked out into the woods. He remembered going up and down the mountain looking for his little zombie girl like it was yesterday, and to be honest, he couldn't help but scour the woods for her now. He knew that she wouldn't be there, but he couldn't help himself.

Hunter seemed unfazed by the whole event. He almost looked as excited as Shelby sounded. How could he be happy? Going back to the cabin that nearly ate him alive with disease, where Matt was shot?

"Hey, what was that?" Lark asked as she pointed out into the woods; Drew couldn't help but crane his neck. He couldn't see anything at first, but then, just as he was about to give up, he noticed the shimmer of pink in the distance. It was beautiful and almost human-shaped. What kind of human, though, would shimmer in the sun like that? There were, after all, a lot of things in this new world that Drew hadn't discovered yet, and after the fiasco that happened the year before, he was more apt to believe in the unknown.

'What is that?" Hunter echoed as he also began to notice the thing in the distance, but everyone's attention turned to the front of the car when Agent Keen announced that they were pulling up to the cabin.

Everyone that Drew knew called this giant house a cabin, but the sheer size of the place begged to differ. It stood three stories tall, and the last time that the men had set foot inside the place, it belonged to one of the town's most well-known historians, Mark Randolph. He was the ringleader of a rather horrible cult that raised a monster from the door at the base of the mountain that separated the five towns from touching. Most people called that mountain the beast... And Drew thought that it was an accurate name, to say the least.

Getting out of the car, Shelby's eyes glittered with excitement. She had wanted to walk the grounds for quite some time. Actually, a few friends had told her of a new flower that had emerged just a few months ago. Her real attraction to the land was for that very flower. She didn't want to seem nosey, but her eyes darted around the building in desperate search for anything that looked out of the ordinary.

"What ya looking for?" Lark asked as Hunter helped the girl out of the car. They hadn't thought of getting any fresh clothes, and even though they had all showered, they were still wearing the night before's battle-torn outfits. Hunter could only imagine what they smelled like. The fairy did reek of death, even before it blew up. Reluctantly, Drew and Keen got out of the car, and they all walked to the front door.

It was a rather warm and sunny day, and Shelby would have done anything just to take a walk around to see the sights and possibly discover new plant life. She had wanted more than anything, even when she was a little girl, to make her very own discovery. It could be a plant or an animal, but just the thought of being in a book or a magazine with something that could make the world a better place lit her heart up like a five-hundred-watt, watt lightbulb.

The door opened, and a rather large man emerged from the inside. Hunter could dare to say that the man was larger than Agent Keen, but wouldn't admit it aloud.

"I'm glad you were able to come in such a hurry. My name is Victor Zanborn, and I am the head of Chapter 151, Guilds of Magic. We have made rooms for your arrival and brought you a few fresh clothes in case you would like to change out of…" The man stopped and sniffed the air a little haphazardly and then stepped back a little. "Well, I can certainly tell you would like to get out of those clothes; I bet Ann can smell you from a mile away."

"Who's Ann?" Lark asked as she shied away from the large man. She was never good with unfamiliar places, especially those with such a sketchy past.

"Ann is a good friend of mine, and I hope she will be one of yours as well. Lark Henson, right?" Lark nodded and calmed down just a bit. Even though the man was large and rather intimidating, he carried a vibe of honesty and comfort.

Everyone went inside and to their respective rooms to clean up and change for the day. No one knew what laid ahead, but they were in it together, and Drew had faith that they would figure it out.

Maybe this time, no one would die. Shelby was the first one out of her room and down the steps. For some reason, she was full of energy and ready for more adventure.

Most people would have been exhausted and even frightened by what had happened the night before, but not Shelby. She had a renewed fearlessness, and it was refreshing. Descending the steps, Shelby let her thin piano fingers glide across the railing. She had a bounce in her step and a smile on her face. The house's foyer was large and open; the light from the bay window bathed the wooden floor. The new polish made it almost look like a thin sheet of glass was over the beautiful, bright flooring.

Shelby walked along the edge of the room, taking in all the beautiful borders and paintings that the guild had put up since their arrival a year before. One photo in particular made her stop and take in what she saw. In this photo, two girls stood; the image was in black and white, but Shelby already knew who she was looking at. Behind them stood a regal-looking man in his mid-forties and a rather fat little fellow in a robe that Shelby imagined was green.

"Wow..." She whispered, "There's no way."

"Yes, they were real." A little meek voice called from the darkened hallway across from the steps. Shelby stepped back, not in fear but more in surprise.

"Who's there?" Shelby asked as she started walking towards the darkness. Shelby saw a little grey hand grab hold of the doorway, but it kept itself inside the threshold of darkness. She could make out the silhouette of a small man, not quite fairy and not quite human. Shelby's mouth dropped, and her eyes widened once she realized who she had come across. "St... Stardock?" She whispered into the darkness.

"Yes, ma'am, you found me. I would suppose the photo you were admiring is that of your family bloodline."

"Pardon me?" Shelby said as she took another step closer. She could hear the footsteps of another person coming from behind Stardock, and another, much larger, frame encompassed that of the little halfling.

"Well, lookie there, Doc, it's ol' Shell... Hey, didn't you say just the other day that if this little feller were real, he would have eaten me for breakfast?" Shelby couldn't help but smile at the sound of the old man's voice and ventured into the dimly lit room with the two of them.

"If he were so inclined," Shelby said with a smirk. "But now that I've met him, I've already become quite fond." She could tell that her kind words touched the little man, and she thought it quite sad because she felt in her heart that he had not been shown much kindness in his long life. "Come!" She said to the two of them and slipped her hand into Stardock's equally long fingers. "We have much to discuss."

"That we do, ma'am," Samuel said as he followed them across the room and down another hallway;

in fact, it was the exact same hallway that Hunter and Andrew had gone the night of the rising. Stardock was leading her into the book room. Finally, before they got to the door of the immense room, Samuel put a cautioned hand on both of their shoulders.

"Are you sure we should be doing this?" Samuel asked, but he already knew the answer to his own question. Shelby was already much more outgoing, and she was unfazed by Stardock's presence. It had already begun, and if they let her go in blind, she would play right into the fairies' hands.

CHAPTER EIGHTEEN

Andrew had made his way to the other side of the third floor, to the door that was marked Head of the Guild. He could hear Victor on the other side of the door talking to someone on the phone, but he quickly got off when he heard Andrew knocking on the door.

"Come in." The man called, and Andrew opened the door, walking through, almost hitting his head on a hanging potted plant by the door.

"Bluebells?" Drew asked as he stopped the swinging plant and walked over to Victor's desk, sitting on the soft chair on the other side of it. "I hope I'm not disturbing you," Andrew said as he began to take in the room. It was almost more of a greenhouse than an office, and Victor could tell Drew was confused.

"Ah, I thought it would be you or the large one that would have come to me first. He gives off, I don't know, police vibes." Victor said as he sat down on the other side of the desk.

"You have good senses. He's an agent for Councilman Howards over in Finch Hollow, but after the incident here in this very house, I would beg to say he got a pretty big promotion." Victor smiled and nodded his head.

"Yes, this place has a pretty weird history, and don't even get me started on the buildings that stood before this one... All on the same foundation." Drew kept looking around at all the flowers hanging about and couldn't help but feel a little claustrophobic.

"What's with all the flowers? You garden?" Victor let out a snorted laugh and leaned back in his chair.

"No, my good man, it's to keep out the fairies." Andrew let out a little snort and then looked around the room further. He had seen a lot of things in his day, and even though he had seen something at the house the night before, he still wasn't one hundred percent sure that the term fairy was correct...

"How do you know that they work? These flowers and the rod iron you have over the doors and windows?" Andrew asked as he leaned back in his seat. For some reason, he felt like he was in some sort of interview... Who knows, maybe he was? Victor laced his fingers together and tilted his head. He was trying to get a fix on the guy but couldn't quite do so.

Just a few hours before, there were three liabilities in town; then two more rolled in. Where did they come from, and what connection did they have with the resurgence? No, something was off, but Victor wasn't sure if it was in his interest or against it.

"Only in theory, which was until Doc turned back into his old self. That was a sight to behold; it almost happened all at once, and I could tell the old fellow was in pain the entire time. It's a shame, really, how it all had to go down."

"Doc?" Drew asked; he had only been in the house a short while, but hadn't seen another soul other than Victor and his friends. How many other people were in the house, and were they to be trusted?

"Never you mind him; right now, we have much to discuss. There are things afoot, things I'm quite sure you and your friends are unaware of." Victor leaned forward once again, laying his eyes square on Drew's. He wanted to make sure that the man's attention was directed at him for the next thing he was about to say because it was particularly important. "I can tell that you are the leader of this group, no matter how recent your entry was to this affair. This means you have to be briefed on what it is that you've actually walked in on."

"And what might that be?" Drew asked.

"Why, my good man, the second wave, the second resurgence."

CHAPTER NINETEEN

Hunter had changed into his new clothes, and even though they didn't quite fit, he thought it was genuinely nice of them to think of the group. They were outsiders in the cabin, even though Hunter and Drew both had horrible encounters there. The thought of what he had seen that night still made his skin crawl, and that was probably why he ventured out into the hallway and made his way to the other rooms on the third floor. He had been distracted by Shelby's excitement on the way up, but now he was left with his thoughts, and they crept through his mind like the ghosts of his long-gone friends.

The first room he entered had to have been Andrew's because he had left his cell phone on the bed and his fedora on the nightstand. Leave it to the old man to forget his lifeline. Hunter couldn't help but smile at the sight of it. He knew how lucky he was to go to work every day and see a friendly face; most people never get to have that.

Shutting the door behind him, he made his way to the next door. He could hear the shower running and thought better than just to barge in. Lifting his hand to knock, he looked down and realized that he was now wearing a short-sleeved shirt. He had tried his best to wear a coat or long sleeves in public after what had happened in this very hall and instinctively covered the scar up with his right hand.

The doctors that he had gone to see told him that a skin graft would work, but no matter how hard they tried, the marks would return within a month. After three failed attempts, Hunter just gave up and started wearing shirts that would cover the giant bite. Andrew had told him not to be ashamed and that he should wear the scar with honor because, after all, he did save the town, if not the entire world, and Hannah was always going to be forever grateful. Somehow, though, that mark haunted him. It took six months before the nightmare passed, and every so often, he would still wake up in a cold sweat.

Getting ready to walk away from the door, he heard the water cut off and the door to the bathroom open and softly shut. He didn't want the person on the other side to know that he was out there; he didn't want either of the girls to think he was a creep, but as he walked away from the door, the floorboard behind him creaked, revealing his presence.

"Hello?" The girl's voice called out, and Hunter knew that hiding or leaving would make him look even more creepy. So he answered back.

"Lark? It's just me; I don't like being alone in this place." There was a silence, and then the door opened up. Lark popped her head out between the crack in the door and smiled. Her red hair was a matted mess on the top of her head; she motioned for him to come inside.

They had left the girl a pair of sweatpants and a grey tee, which she had haphazardly put on, and even though they were extremely small, they still hung loosely upon Lark's tiny frame. The neck of the shirt, in particular, would slide off one shoulder or the other, and Hunter could tell that it was a little bit annoying for her.

"Anything you want to talk about?" Lark asked as she sat down on the edge of the bed. Hunter took a few steps into the room and glanced around. Thankfully, this was not one of the rooms he had been in a year before.

"Not particularly; where do you think the others went?" Hunter said, shifting his feet, his eyes darting around the room. He was beginning to realize what William had gone through when they had to go back to Claire's apartment. How he must have felt knowing that the person who had attacked and held him hostage was gone, but the ghost of her would always haunt the place where it had happened. He hadn't noticed that he was still covering the scar with his hand, but Lark had.

"More than likely, Shelby is outside wandering around, being the fearless nature girl she is. I wouldn't know about the others."

"No, I don't suppose you would." He said with a smile. Lark pulled the oversized shirt over one shoulder, only to see it slide off the other.

"This shirt is driving me nuts." She said a little nervously. Hunter smiled and took another step closer to her. "You don't have to stand all the way over there; you can sit with me." Hunter nodded and sat down next to the girl.

"I'm sorry, sometimes I let my nervousness get the better of me. After all the things that have happened, I guess I've been distracted enough not to realize how much I really like you." Lark smiled and put her hand over the one covering the scar.

"I like you too, so you don't have to hide anything from me." Hunter looked over at the girl, and he could tell that her words were genuine. "Look, I will do you one better; if you show me yours, I'll show you mine." Without another word, Lark took her unoccupied hand and pulled the neck of her shirt down to expose a long, jagged scar. It had red lines running through it, almost like road rash. Hunter thought for a minute that the scar was fresh. Opening his mouth to ask about it, Lark just shook her head. "Don't bother asking because I don't know. I have no memory of it, and to be honest, I'm almost relieved. It looks gnarly, and I bet whatever caused it was even worse."

Hunter knew that he couldn't back out of it now. He hated the way that the scar made him look and the way that it healed. He was thankful for his life and would always owe Keen a great debt, but the scar... It would always be a reminder. Taking a deep breath, Hunter released his hand from the scar, exposing it to Lark, whose eyes widened in wonderment. "Oh, my..." She started.

"I know, it's gross," Hunter said, hanging his head. He began to inch away from the girl, but she tightened her grip on his hand and inched closer. Taking her eyes off the scar, she laid them on his face and gave him another smile.

"Tell me all about it. I want to know everything."

In good old-fashioned Keen style, the agent had slipped out of the back door of the three-story house. The same door, in fact, that he had lock-picked a year before. He didn't quite have the same fears as Hunter and felt the need to walk the perimeter of the land just to see what was out there. He hadn't been outside long when he began to feel eyes upon him. He made a three-sixty circle and put his hand on his gun, but he could see nothing out of the ordinary.

"Who's there?" Keen said in a commanding voice, but no one responded. Maybe it was just his imagination, but he didn't think so. After all these years working as a special agent, he had a knack for telling when someone was stalking him.

Turning his back to the cabin, Agent Keen continued to walk in silence. He was pretending to look around the property, but now he was much more interested in who or what was following him.

Ann Key was right on the man's trail, hiding in plain sight, darting behind a tree as the man continued to walk around the woods. The large man amused her. She didn't trust the newcomers yet and knew she would have to keep an eye on them, especially the girls. She could feel that they would be in trouble. Again, the large man put his hand on his weapon as he turned around at the edge of the mountain and began to make his way back to the cabin.

"You know, if I had wanted to, I could have easily pushed you right off, and your little friends would have been none the wiser." Jerking in the direction of the voice he had heard, Agent Keen came face to face with Ann Key Bishop.

Not a lot of humans outside of the guild had laid eyes on her face, and she was less than happy about his response. Agent Keen didn't flinch; he didn't move; he just stood there for a moment, assessing the situation and keeping a twitchy hand over his pistol.

"Who are you?" He asked, relaxing a little. She could tell that he had evaluated the situation and assumed she was a non-threat.

"You, first." She said as she motioned for them to start walking back to the cabin. Slowly, they began through the thin foliage; Keen could hear the call of the whooping cranes that had begun to migrate for the season and breathed in the fresh air that encompassed them. Ann's skin sparkled in the sunlight, and he could tell that she was also drinking in nature and all its bounty.

"My name is Keen, Agent Keen of the Finch Hollow Secret Service. I'm here to help my friends Hunter Williams and Andrew Bower. I'm sure sense, you must be native to these parts, are aware of the happenings inside those walls." Ann nodded and put her hands behind her back.

"I am quite aware of the first resurgence. I am not, though, so sure about your participation in such an event." Keen nodded as they continued through the woods.

"The three of us had to stop and destroy the Beast and its counterparts. With the help of a few others, that's exactly what we did." Ann stopped and turned her sights to the man, who did so in turn.

"You? You and those two behind the walls of our guild participated in the de-throning of the beast? The first resurgence?" Keen nodded and began to walk towards the house once more. "I would surely like to hear about how that came to pass."

"Oh, I am most certain you will, and at great length. I do not doubt that everyone will be fully informed before the night's end." Something in the distance caught Ann's eye, and she darted off in another direction. "Where are you going?" Agent Kenn asked, but she had returned almost as quickly as she had gone.

"They've been here; I don't know how they keep slipping through my spells, but those damn witches have returned, which could only mean one thing." Officer Keen looked down at what had caught Ann's attention. In her hand, she held a flower, not just any flower, but a shiny, mesmerizing flower. One that Agent Keen almost couldn't take his eyes off of. He wanted, more than anything, to take the flower from the woman's hand, but knew that it was against better judgment. By the look on her face, this flower was probably a really bad sign, even though its vibrant blue petals danced magically in the wind, and the little red freckles on each of them created a childlike happiness inside Keen that he had not felt in years.

"What are we looking at?" Keen asked as he reached out instinctively, but Ann pulled the flower back away from him and gave him a warning stare.

"These, my large friend, are called Moonshadows and grow where the witches dwell. If you find one of these, they cannot be too far behind."

"When you say witches?" Keen asked but didn't have to finish his words.

"Mercy's sisters have come to collect. We have hidden her for far too long; I knew this day would come... I was just hoping that we would have been further along than we are."

"Further along in what?" Keen asked as they approached the house.

"On what exactly the sisters want with her."

CHAPTER TWENTY

The sun had come up and then set behind the cabin at Eagles Nest. Everyone had retired for the evening, all that is, except for Shelby, who quite enjoyed walking the darkened halls and listening to the crickets right on the other side.

Samuel and Stardock had told her all about the Mad Nobleman and who she could quite possibly be. It fascinated her to be so close to history, to have any kind of magic in her blood, to wear the crown of the fairies possibly. Who wouldn't want that?

Something shimmered off in the distance, beckoning her from another room. It shimmered in the moonlight like a tiny title wave of blue and red. She thought she could hear the tinkling of bells in the distance. Was she dreaming? Her heart pounded harder with every step she took. She could feel her pulse quicken, reaching out a gingered hand to the thing under the glass dome.

"I wouldn't do that if I were you," Stardock said as he stepped out from the shadows and into the moonlight. Shelby jumped a little and let out a little scream. Covering her mouth with both of her hands, she turned to face the little man, who had his hands on his hips like an angry father catching his daughter sneaking in after curfew.

"Stardock!" Shelby exclaimed in a heated whisper, "You can't just sneak up on people like that!" Doc's stance softened as he walked over to the girl.

"What you're looking at under the dome, that's a Moon-shadow flower, and those things aren't very nice. I can't even touch the thing without feeling a little woozy. Ann is the only one who can."

"What makes her so special?" Shelby said with a little scoff. Her attention fell back onto the flower. She had never seen such a thing in all her life. Was this the chance to discover a new plant? Was this Moon-shadow something new? She couldn't be certain, but she knew that she had to get her hands on more of them.

"You met her; you all have; you know what makes her special, Shelby." Stardock could tell that he had lost her attention again and took a step closer. "Shell?"

"Where could I get my hands on these? Safely, of course..." She said, waving a hand in the air before Stardock had a chance to caution her about the flower's extraordinary gifts. At first, Stardock didn't say a word, but when Shelby turned her gaze at him, he could see the crazed look in her eyes.

As much as the seals had spoken of a Southpaw woman rising up and helping the fairies, it also told of her wrath, and Doc didn't want any part of it.

"The meadows, the one that houses the mother tree, I've been told that the witches convene there amongst the Starshallows and Moon-shadows and eat of the fruit the mother bears before the moon is at its highest. That is how they get their powers, and that is where you can find the flowers." Squatting down and putting her chin on the table that housed the flower, Shelby thought for a moment, almost unable to take her eyes off the petals that seemed to sing to her, to beckon her to their meadow.

"Then that's where we will go this very night."

"But..." Stardock said it was too late. Shelby had taken the poor man's hand, and they were ripping through the cabin, snatching up a few supplies and hijacking the keys to Drew's old beater that he had haphazardly left on the table by the front door.

Lark had fallen asleep earlier than everyone else; after what had happened the night before, she had felt nervous to sleep alone and had invited Hunter to crash on the couch in her room. He had eagerly agreed because he knew that it would make her feel safe, and he would do almost anything to be close to the woman, even if it meant sleeping on a lumpy couch. They were both so soundly asleep that they didn't hear the squeal of the bad belt in the yellow hooptie, and Hunter couldn't see the distress in Lark's eyes as she fell back into the black, inky nothing that she had emerged from the night before.

Again, the girl sat up on the cold, invisible floor, wrapping her arms across her chest. Everything was the same as it had been the night before, except this time, there was a black candle in what Lark could only describe as the middle of the nothing. A single blue flame danced upon its wick and made the room flush with small white flecks. Lark felt as if she were in the middle of outer space.

"Where is this place?" She whispered to herself. Getting to her feet, she slowly walked the short distance to the candle and instinctively looked inside of the flame. She could see the willow tree and the flowers from the field where she used to write, and she became homesick for the simpler times. She wanted more than anything just to go home and forget everything that had happened, everything that is, except for Hunter.

"I know you want to go home; all you have to do is think about it and follow the flame." The same soothing voice from the night before echoed around the room. She could feel the goosebumps rising from her skin, and the room began to shift. She could feel the floor spin from underneath her, and she began to fall through the nothing, floating or falling; she couldn't be for certain... She couldn't tell up from down, and she could feel the nothing beginning to fill her lungs.

Grabbing and clawing at her throat, the girl began to gag and choke. What did this woman want with her?

"Please," She wheezed, "let me go." She could hear the laughter in the woman's voice; her soothing tone had dark-seeded, angry undertones.

"The way you let us go, to fight alone, to face our father alone. No, I don't believe we will." Further still, Lark began to spiral; she could feel the life force leaving her body as her eyes began to roll back into her head and shut for the last time.

"Lark?" She could barely make out the muffled sound of Hunter on the other side of the dark.

"Hunter?" Lark whispered into the nothing. She could feel his warmth enveloping her, protecting her, and the breath entered her lungs once more. The feeling of spiraling out of control began to stop, and the tone in the woman's voice began to change.

"No, you cannot do this again, Mercy! No, NO!" Lark's eyes fluttered open, and she was once again at the cabin in her bed, but Hunter was not on the couch. He had rushed to her side, scooping her up from her own personal hell, and held her in his arms until the sound of his voice had carried her home.

Looking up at the man, she smiled and put a cold hand against his cheek.

"My knight." She whispered. Leaning down, he placed a gentle kiss on her forehead.

"For as long as you need." It was at that moment that Keen and Samuel busted through the door and began looking around at the situation.

"Oh, thank God only one of them ventured off," Samuel said as he began to rub his forehead.

"What do you mean?" Hunter asked as he got to his feet. Lark wrapped the blankets around her tightly. Without Hunter to keep her warm, she could feel the cold darkness begin to creep in all over.

"Looks like Shelby ran off with Andrew's car. We are looking over the house for any other missing people." Keen said, motioning for Hunter to come closer.

"Stardock is missing too," Drew said as he and Ann began the walk down the hallway. Lark began to scratch her head as she thought about the dream she had before, about the blue flame and what she had seen through it.

"I think I know where she's going." Lark blurted out. Discarding the blankets, she slid out of bed and put on a pair of tennis shoes that she had found in the bathroom earlier that day. "If I'm right, we have to move now."

"Wait... Wait a second, darlin'," Samuel said, putting up a cautioned hand. "Can't go running out of here, guns ablaze; where do you think she might be?"

"The meadows, in Shadows End, where I used to write my stories... There's a tree there."

"The mother tree. She must be getting called to her roots... This can't be good." Ann said as she brushed past Drew, who was taking it all in.

"Well, what are we supposed to do?" Hunter asked as he made his way back to the couch. Throwing his shoes on. He knew that this was going to be another long night. Hopefully, it would end without anyone getting hurt.

"We have to find Victor. Tell him what is going on." Drew said, but the look on Ann's face told him that it would be easier said than done.

"We can't, at least not for a while. You are right, though; he has to be told. We should stay behind and wait for his arrival."

"Where did he go?" Samuel asked, turning to face the Witch.

"You know where..." She responded as they all made their way out into the hallway and to the front door. Lark was the last person out of the bedroom, and for some distinctive reason, she felt the need to grab the red necklace and slip it into the pocket of her sweatpants. Something told her that she would need it... That it was still important, that under no circumstances should Shelby get ahold of it.

Ann thought for a second and pointed to Drew.

"You and I will stay here and wait for Victor to return. It might be a while, but it has to be us."

"Why?" Drew asked. He didn't like to be the one just to sit around and wait, especially when he brought himself down there to help his friend.

Now, he thought, everyone else had been doing a better job at assisting Hunter than he had.

"She doesn't do so hot in the moonlight," Keen said as he nodded at Ann. Ann nodded back, so Keen continued. "The best way to describe it. She is a sun creature, and if she's exposed too long, she could burn up."

"I thought it was somethin' like that," Samuel said as he shifted his weight. "You're like a reverse fairy; those little boogers burst into flames at a single ray of sunlight. Magnificent to watch; just keep your distance, though; their blood is like acid."

"Keen, you and Sam go to the meadows. Don't waste any time. I'm not sure what she's got planned, but we have to stop her at all costs. I can tell you two are our best fighters, and you may need those skills to knock out a fairy or two on your way." Smiling over at Ann, Samuel tipped his hat.

"It's damn good to be back in business, ma'am. I will tell the big guy where to go." He said as he quickly followed Keen out of the front door. They slipped into the SUV and drove away without another word. Hunter and Lark were about to follow them when Ann stood in front of the door.

"Not you two, not yet." Lark felt a surge of anger wash over her. It was an uncomfortable and surprising feeling. She was not often angered, but tonight was different. Without her, they wouldn't have known where to go. Her sisters were close, and she thought that was where they would be... Why was she to stay behind like a little baby?

"Why?" Lark yelled. She tried to push past Ann, but Hunter wrapped a strong arm around her waist, picking her up. Moving her away from the Witch, he looked down at Lark.

"We have to understand that Ann has more experience than us on these matters. I trust her." Hunter said calmly.

"You don't trust me?" Lark responded meekly, and at that moment, Hunter's heart broke just a little.

"I do; it's just that I couldn't even bear the thought of you getting hurt... or worse." At the sound of logic, Lark began to calm down and looked over at the beautiful creature in the doorway. Ann, for however little amount of time, had never steered anyone wrong, and tonight would, most likely, be no different.

"So, what's the plan?" Drew asked as he stepped beside his friends. He didn't want to seem too eager, but he felt a little bit of happiness that he would get to fight beside his old friend once again. Maybe he was there for a reason.

"Mercy... I mean, Lark, you will get a chance to see your sisters. I know that's why you wanted to go there tonight. Have they been talking to you? Has that begun already?" Lark nodded at Ann and crossed her arms around her chest. The thought of the nothingness brought chills across her skin like a piercing snow drift.

"I don't think they will be there; I know it... I saw it." Ann tilted her head to one side and squinted her eyes at the girl. Her raven hair pushed back behind her pointy ears, the one blond bit making the blue in her eyes twinkle in the dwindling overhead light.

"You SAW it? Oh, my, this isn't good. Where did you see it, Lark?"

"When I sleep, I go to this... Dark place, and one of the sisters talks to me."

"Melinda..." Ann whispered into the air. "She's pulling you through the veil, through the nothing... You can't survive long in there. How did you get out?" Lark looked up at the tall lady, holding herself a little tighter.

"I don't know, the first time there was a tear in the dark and a long, creepy hand pulled me out, that sucked because when I came to, I was so sick, throwing up this black junk. Tonight, though, tonight was different. I was even deeper into the nothingness, and I heard Hunter; he saved me."

"You? Saved her from the void?" Drew asked with a smile. "Pretty badass." Hunter blushed a bit but couldn't help admiring his friend's attempt at lightening the mood.

"We have to hurry. If she's pulling you through the veil, it will only be a matter of time before they come here to take you. It's been proven that as long as you have Hunter, they cannot kill you through the darkness."

"Wait, Wait! Kill her?" Hunter said, instinctively grabbing Lark and pulling her close to his chest.

"We have to hurry. I wasn't sure before, but now I have no doubt the sisters want you dead, Lark. We did all we could to protect you... To shroud you from them, but in the end, we knew this day would come. I just had hoped we would have known more. The why behind their malicious intent."

The four of them made their way into the back room, where the blue flower still sat under the glass. Its beauty resounded within the emptiness of the room. The men thought it was the most striking flower either of them had laid eyes on, but Lark couldn't stand the sight of it.

"What is that wretched little weed?" Lark asked, recoiling a little.

"I figured you would say that," Ann said as she took the glass top off.

"You're going to need it. In fact, you're going to have to eat it."

CHAPTER TWENTY-ONE

Keen and Samuel had just left the mountain and began their trek through town. Samuel knew it wasn't more than a twenty-minute drive, and his partner seemed very intent on the road in front of him.

"So, um... Is there anything we need to discuss before we get to the old stomping grounds?" Samuel asked, running his hands over his guns. Those things had been in the family as long as he could remember, and with a few tweaks, his dad had been able to make iron-tipped bullets just for the fairy folk. It was a time-consuming task making the bullets himself, but worth it when they exploded mid-flight. All he had left tonight were three in each of his pistols.

"Not particularly; I spoke with Ann about a lot of things today while we were together, fascinating woman. She briefed me on the situation at hand. How Shelby could be the leader of this revolution, there's just one thing I don't understand." Keen stopped at the last light in town before they reached the long stretch of field, driving right to the meadows.

"What's that partner?" Samuel said with a smile. For some reason, Keen couldn't shake the feeling that Samuel couldn't be trusted. It just didn't sit right.

"The third seal, the hint that brought the resurgence tablets to light. Her body will be made whole by the connection of her roots. Her roots were against the fairy uprising... Why would she want to help them now?" Samuel sat back in his seat a little further and ran a hand across his five o'clock shadow.

"The best we can figure is that when Faith was poisoned by Corrowin when they both were to die, it created some sort of bond. Her giant protected her to the very end, even when she became the mother tree." Keen was silent for a moment and then looked over at Samuel, perplexed.

"You mean to tell me that..." Before the man had a chance to say another word, a loud thump hit the driver's side of the SUV so hard that it lifted onto two wheels for a moment and then came back down with a resounding thud.

"What the hell?!?!?" Keen said as he tried to correct his steering. Once he had regained control of the vehicle, Keen turned the bright beams in hopes of seeing what exactly had hit them.

"Damn, fairies," Samuel muttered as he pointed to the three figures flying toward the car like fat, ugly hummingbirds.

"What the..." Keen's eyes widened in wonderment; last year, it was zombies, and now the fairy apocalypse? It was always something with those boys. Trying to miss the onslaught, Keen swerved to the left a little, but his front tire bumped up against a fallen tree hidden in the tall grass, causing the car to jackknife into a large field of corn.

Rolling over onto its side, the SUV capsized in the sea of yellow, but the two men managed to crawl out from the driver's side door with little more than a few cuts to their names.

"Looks like the car is toast," Keen said as he watched the front of the SUV begin to smoke a little.

"Um, we should probably get the Hell out of here," Samuel said as he began to back away from Keen.

"We could probably make it on foot in an hour," Keen responded, but the look on Samuel's face told him that Shelby was the last thing on his mind at the moment. The twinkling of bells in the background reminded him of what Ann had told him during lunch, about how the fairies would hide in the shadows and attract children to them with the sounds of bells and kind laughter. They had even been able to throw their voices to make themselves sound like they were somewhere else.

Slowly drawing his gun, Samuel pointed it above Keen's head.

"Wow, wow, easy there, cowboy," Keen said as he began to draw his own weapon. Cocking the gun, Samuel squinted one eye and tilted his head back.

"Nice and slow, Keen, walk towards me." The agent could hear the children's laughter, and the bells were getting louder. He knew that it was now or never; drawing his own weapon, the man spun around and fired two bullets into the sky. Letting out a pained cry, the little monster fell, spraying acidic blood across the field, marking towers of corn with black ooze. One of Keen's bullets had gone straight through his chest, but it did little to slow him down.

"You'll never make it to the meadows. We won't let you." The other two fairies emerged from either side of the men, flanking them, giving them little space to go. Pointing the gun at the injured monster, Samuel took a step forward,

"Good thing I got enough of these to wipe the three of you out." The monster smiled and took another step toward the gunslinger. He could hear hissing coming from the larger fairy to his left.

"She's almost there; I can sense her." The third monster said as he lashed out at Keen; in a flash, it was on top of him, throwing its claws at the man's face. It was all he could do to keep the fairy from taking his pound of flesh.

"Get off of him!" Samuel yelled as he ran towards Keen, but was stopped by the larger fairy who rushed him, head-butting him in the kidney. With a loud oof, Samuel went down hard on his belly. The injured fairy jumped up and down with excitement, clapping his hands together with glee.

Everything was so distracting that no one noticed the wind beginning to pick up, that the SUV started to smoke even more, or even that sparks had begun to flit through the air from the hood of the capsized car. No, everyone was far too engaged in the fight.

First, Keen had found his footing, grappling on the ground with the deceptively strong little man. Outweighing the fairy by at least two hundred pounds, Keen managed to roll him over onto his back and pin his arms to the dusty ground.

"Gotcha' now, little gross thing..." Looking over to his left, he could see his pistol lying on its side. How was he to get to it without letting the monster go? He knew he couldn't, so he barrel-rolled as fast as he could. It took the odd-shaped beast a moment to get to his feet, and that was long enough; as it approached Agent Keen, he could hear Samuel in the background.

"The head hit it in the head!" Lying on his back, he aimed for the monster's head as it lunged towards him, claws up, mouth open and unhinged, exposing yellow jagged razorblade teeth. Firing off a third round, the bullet smashed through the little one's skull, leaving a golf ball-sized hole at the exit point. Stopping in its tracks, it blinked twice and then fell at Keen's feet, squelching blood onto the dry soil.

Samuel had tried to roll over, but the little fat demon had ascended onto his back, rendering him motionless.

"Want to see what we do to people like you... Well, people in general." It said, as it opened its mouth, a long, forked tongue emerged; it would have been terrifying to see if Sam wasn't on his back.

"Oh, I'm sure you are very scary, but all I can see is the dirt and a few bugs. I wonder if this farmer has an ant infestation." Sam knew that fairies were vain, and it would let the man go just long enough to watch his very own demise; he had, after all, killed his fair share. Screaming in anger, the fat one rolled off of the gunslinger, and that was all that the man needed. Rolling onto his back and pulling the other gun from his hip, he shot a single round into the creature. Screaming out into the night, he began to shake and pop, taking off in flight and then falling back onto the ground with a thud. Its little eyes bulged in shock, and then they popped right out of its little head.

"She will make you pay!" The little injured fairy screamed, lunging at Keen, who was still on the ground and this one wasted no time, taking a huge bite out of Keen's ankle.

"Aaaaaa!" He screamed in pain, drawing Sam's attention to the agent. Leaping to his feet, he aimed at the fairy and shot. It let go of the agent's leg but sprayed black blood into the open wound.

"Oh, shit, oh shit, oh shit." Sam began as both of the fairies exploded all around them, leaving them in a circle of black oil.

"Yeah, that's what I said too when I was watching from over there." A voice said; the two men had gotten to their feet and retrieved their guns looking over at the odd little man. He had a yellow bowl of popcorn, munching away.

"Who the hell are you?" Samuel asked as he began to hold the gun at the new person.

"Me? I'm nobody, but you can call me Raz; most people do... Well, it's either that or GET OFF MY LAWN WEIRDO! Raz is shorter."

Keen lifted his hand and looked over at the little man.

"I think I know him; I don't know why... I just do."

"Well, just thought I would tell you, just a suggestion though, that your car is gonna pop, aaaannnnd, well, you're surrounded by..." Raz motioned all around them. Sam's eyes widened at the realization of the danger they were in now.

"We gotta go, NOW!" Grabbing Keen's shoulder, the two men rushed past Raz as the SUV went up in flames. "Aren't you coming with us?" Samuel asked as the flames got higher. He knew that once the fire hit the body's flesh, they would go up like mini nukes. They had to make as much space between them and the fire as humanly possible.

"Nah," Raz called back, "I'm almost out of popcorn."

CHAPTER TWENTY-TWO

Misty had wandered into the meadows once again by herself. The moon was almost at its highest, and she thought for just a second that, in the far distance, near the weird old tree, she could see hints of flowing red hair. Would the girls still be there? Would she have to let the blood flow once again? She certainly hoped so.

Approaching the willow, Misty could feel the warm night air kiss her skin, the wand in one hand and a satchel in the other, prepared to snatch up as many Starshallow flowers as she could hold.

Kneeling by the tree, she picked one flower after the other, making certain that the subtle differences weren't present. She had filled her bag halfway before the sound of a woman's voice stopped her from her chore.

"What you gonna do with all those pretty flowers?" Turning to see who was speaking to her, there stood a tall blond woman, there was nothing too special that Misty could see. Pretty, blond… not unlike the girl he had killed in the tub a few years ago. Misty smiled at the lady and put the satchel down at her feet.

"You don't happen to be a pesky little witch, do you?" Shelby smiled back at the little girl and shook her head.

"No, we left that one at the house," Misty smirked and couldn't help but admire the woman's boldness. Maybe in another life, they could have been friends, but not tonight. Tonight, Misty got to gain power, and tonight, the goblins would leave her alone… Or so she thought.

Shelby may have been out of her mind with mania, but she wasn't insane, and she wasn't stupid. She could smell the blood lust on the little girl, and even though she couldn't have been more than seventeen, she had lived. The large, ragged scar on the right side of her face told her that much.

"You want to kill me, don't you?" Shelby asked as she began to pace the circumference of the tree, letting her hand slide around the trunk like a maypole.

"You remind me of someone." Misty hissed as she slid the wand into the loop of her pants and pulled out the stone knife from her pocket. "Come here, and let me give you a makeover." Shelby laughed as she rounded the corner of the tree. She had a piece of fruit in her hand. Taking a bite, Shelby's eyes began to glow under the branches of the old willow. Not blue or green, but the brightest white light that Misty had ever seen. Almost as if two thousand watts of electricity had entered her eye sockets. Misty shielded her face from the offending light with the hand that held the knife. Shelby laughed as she started to walk towards the girl.

"Just because I am not a witch, you think I wield no power?" Misty's eyes began to widen in wonderment as she happened upon Shelby's bare feet and the roots that had grown through them. "It would seem, little one, that you are not the only person to have misjudged my motives." Misty could hear the tinkling of bells all around her. But how? How could the fairies get into the meadows? Again, she could hear the Manic laughter of the crazy tree lady. "I let them in; they are, after all, here to protect me."

The first fairy swooped down, slashing at the girl's face with a nasty clawed hand. Misty fell to the ground on her back and swung the knife blindly into the air.

"What the fuck!" She yelled, "Deaththorne, you bitch! I thought you had these shit's under control!" Deaththrone didn't answer because he had his hands full on the other side of the meadow. Again, the fairy advanced, and again, Misty swung wildly into the night, barely grazing the thing with her blade. A few drops of blood dripped down onto her arm, and she screamed in pain as it immediately drilled holes through her flesh.

The smell of rot and mold filled her nostrils, and it was enough to make the girl rage out even harder. Jumping to her feet, Misty snatched the wand from her belt loop and pointed it at the little ghoul. "FIRE!" She screamed. The splinter in her hand began to tingle. She had gotten it the night before and had forgotten about it until now, but something was definitely happening. The tip of the wand began to turn green, like the moss in the swamp, and a small diamond-shaped mass grew from the end. Energy began to fill the mass with foggy grey swirls.

Both of the girls had stopped for a moment; even the fairy had no idea what was going on, that was until a bolt of light flew from the tip of the wand and hit the flying grey maneater, lighting him up midair, causing a rather large fireball that was there almost as quickly as it vanished. Again, she heard the tinkling of bells flanking her from the front, and again, she reached up with her wand, but this time, the fairy outsmarted her and snatched it from her hand.

"What are you going to do now, beast lady?" The thing yelled back with a cackle. Lifting the blade, Misty threw it, catching the lacky in the back of the head, driving the blade deep into its skull. Falling face down in the thick grass, the girl retrieved the wand and kicked the rest of the knife through the fairy's head. She knew to back away before the explosion.

Misty had a moment to look down at her wound; the fiery pain had stopped, and now there was only numbness around the two deep holes in her arm. It wasn't the worst wound she had ever received, not by far, but it still bothered her as to how she had gotten it.

"Who gave you Mara's wand?" The tall blond lady asked. Misty looked over at Shelby and knew that she had better get out of there. The roots that had begun at her feet had made their way up her legs, and she wore one of them around her waist like a belt.

"Who... who the hell are you?" Misty asked as she inched closer to the woman. She had to retrieve the bag.

"My vessel is named Shelby, but I am the Qhizyja. The tower of the South, and guider of the darkness." At this point, Shelby had begun to float a few inches from the ground, and to Misty, with all those roots going through her, she almost looked like a parade balloon.

Snatching the flower bag, Misty darted towards the north side of the meadow, where Deaththorne had left her... but Shelby was having none of that. With a battle cry, a wand of her own formed from her left wrist, almost like a horn, and on the end of it stood a crystalline ball that could have been Mother of Pearl. White smoke blew through it like the old dustbowl in the Shadows End Mirror world. Who knows, maybe it was its own world. Holding her hand out in a stop motion, she aimed for the little girl, who was bobbing and weaving through the tall grass. Pure energy blasts began to fly from Shelby's wand, missing her by mere inches. Misty couldn't help but feel like she was in the middle of a war movie, and even though she was frightened, it had been a long time since she had felt so alive.

Stumbling to the ground, the girl almost lost her bag; staggering back, she snatched it up but nearly fell down at what she saw next. The tall blond woman was standing right in front of her with a menacing smile. Her glowing eyes had begun to dim, but the power behind them had not wavered.

"Who gave you Mara's wand, little one?" Mouth open in terror, Misty made one last attempt at making it out of the meadow; with the leap that would make any jackrabbit jealous, she barely saved her own skin as an energy bolt followed her to the edge of the field, but was stopped short but what could have only be described as a forcefield. Screaming out in anger, the Qhizyja floated back to the tree, head held low on her chest.

Once she released her army, things would all change, and the balance would be destroyed. For that, she would make certain. Lying down at the base of the tree, she began to sing a song she had never heard before, and she drifted into a dark and empty dreamland.

CHAPTER TWENTY-THREE

Hunter had paced the floor of his room for quite a while. What Ann had asked Lark to do was dangerous, and she was still mulling it over. Drew was downstairs awaiting Victor's arrival, and there had still been no sign of the man. Where on Earth could he have gone? Ann seemed to know, but she wasn't telling. Drew couldn't quite figure out if it was from loyalty or shame.

There was a knock on Hunter's door, and he opened it to see Lark on the other side. She didn't wait for the man to say anything, wrapping her arms around his neck, then pulled away, kissing him. Looking into his eyes, Lark knew that it might be the last time she was ever to see him the same. She knew that the spell would unlock all the memories of who she was, her past, and possibly her magic. It frightened her to understand that the person she had been for the last twenty-three years might not be the person she really was at all. Was there anything more horrifying than not knowing who you really were?

"You've made your decision, haven't you?" Hunter said quietly. It was hard for him to look at her, not because he was angry, but because he couldn't bear to become any more attached to the woman than he already was. What was he going to do with himself if he lost her just as fast as he found her?

"Yes," She said, burying her face in his chest and breathing him in. His embrace might have been the most comforting place she had ever been, and now she had to leave it for the unknown, to fight her sisters, and for what? She hadn't the foggiest. "I have to know who I am, Hunter. I have to find out, and I have to keep them from hurting you or anyone else."

"Last time I checked, love, they were trying to kill you. I couldn't imagine why." Lark pulled away and smiled at him. Kissing him one last time, she walked down the hall and vanished into Ann's room, where she had been waiting to start the transformation.

Lark closed the door behind her and took a look over at what Ann had done to the room. She motioned for the girl to come closer. The blue flower was in the room next to a table covered in a white cloth.

"Here," Ann said, handing Lark a white gown. It was sheer and silky. In all her days alive, Lark would never have picked something like this to wear, even to bed, but she did as she was told and then sat down on the table, waiting for further instructions.

"Is this going to hurt?" She asked as she ran her hand across the deep scar on her shoulder. She thought that maybe, just maybe, the scar was part of the other ritual, the one that had caused her to forget, and if they had to do it once, then...

"My dear," Ann said as she took the top off the flower. The room began to fill with a pungent odor; Lark thought it smelled like pomegranates or some other tropical fruit. Ann, on the other hand, thought it smelled of old magic, the most dangerous kind. "Pain is subjective, and I haven't performed this spell on myself, so I wouldn't even know how to explain what you will be going through." Lark nodded; she didn't know what kind of answer she was looking for, to be honest. Maybe she was just looking for hope.

Lying down on the table, Lark closed her eyes as the ceremony began. Lifting the flower over her head, she could hear Ann begin to chant. At first, she thought it was in another language, but as the

Witch continued, she began to understand what she was saying.

"Take the flesh of my kindred and reunite them with my memories; take my soul and unshroud it from the folds of immunity." Lark began to feel uneasy, and she didn't think it was from the spell itself but from the cryptic words that emerged from the woman's mouth.

"What..."

"Shhh," Ann said as she continued the chant, and just as Lark was about to get up off the table, an intense pressure began to pour down upon her body, and her mouth opened wide. Ann placed the flower inside of Lark's mouth, and she couldn't help but swallow the thing whole.

At first, she couldn't breathe; it was almost as if she were back in nothing, gasping for her life, but she couldn't move; she could see everything around her. A single tear rolled down her face as she looked at Ann with pleading eyes. "Don't worry, my dear; it will all be over soon." Ann ran her long pink fingers through the girl's red hair, which had begun to curl and grow in length. The scar on her shoulder began to grow warmer and warmer until it felt as if hot coals were inside her. Lark's lungs began to feel as if they were going to burst, but just as she was about to pass out, the flower's hold released, and she sat up on the table, gasping for air, putting both hands around her neck.

"What, what happened... I don't remember anything." Lark said, looking over at Ann, but then she began to look down at herself, understanding that she wasn't exactly the same person she had walked in as.

Her red hair had become curly and long, waving down her back, almost like a waterfall of red silk; her skin, even though it had been pale, to begin with, was virtually pearl white; she knew that she had grown in height as well because the table that was far too long when she got on a few moments ago was now just large enough. What did Ann do to her?

"In due time, my child. Lay back and wait for it." Lark wanted to resist, but a wave of dizziness came over her, and she thought better of it. Putting a slender, pale hand up to her head, Lark began to swallow hard and then fell back onto the table with a thud. Her eyes fluttered shut, and she was out like a light, wafting through the memories she should have had with her sisters and the truth about why they wanted her dead.

CHAPTER TWENTY-FOUR

The story of Melinda Monroe is a sad one, one that doesn't get nearly as much attention as that of her counterpart, Merry Belle, but as I have said before, they both deserve to be told. Melinda is the oldest of the three, and as such, her mother always expected her to take care of Merry Belle when she was away on business, and by business, her mother meant tending to the needs of their father, Murdock.

Melinda had always been jealous of her sister's beauty, even though she knew that she herself was ravishing and could get whomever she wanted just by flashing a smile. There was something about Merry Belle, though, something that she couldn't put her finger on, and it drove the girl crazy.

Then Merry Belle had to do the unthinkable; she had to get a man. It wasn't that Melinda wanted him because that wasn't the case. Once Rigney became a regular part of Merry's life, Melinda never got to see her sister, and even though she was jealous of her, they were also best friends.

For the first year of the romance, Melinda waited and watched as her sister swooned over the boy, practically drooling over him. It made Melinda sick at times to see such affection, and then, one day, Melinda seized the opportunity to ruin her sister's relationship for the last time.

Melinda had had enough of her mother's companionship and pretended to be sick, and on that day, Merry Belle and Rigney Lancaster decided to venture into the Monroe residence. Melinda knew they did this on occasion, but honestly didn ' t expect it to happen today; it was almost serendipitous.

Sneaking from her room, she ventured down the hall and waited for Merry Belle to leave. Possibly to get something to drink, but it didn't really seem to matter at the time because Melinda took on the form of her sister and walked into the room to seduce the man lying in bed by the large bay window.

"Rigney, I'm ready." She said in her best Merry voice. At first, the man smiled and looked over at the girl, but then his expression changed.

"Wait, there's something about you. There's something different." He began, but before he had the chance to say anything else, Melinda was on top of him, kissing him, and when he went to push her off, Merry Belle entered the room in a rage. His hands on Melinda's hips looked like an embrace of passion, and the girl had changed form once again into her true self.

Leaping from the bed, she ran past her sister, knowing full well what she had done. You see, Rigney had done nothing wrong and was simply punished for loving the wrong girl, who was a member of the wrong family. It had taken years for Merry Belle to forgive her sister for the betrayal fully, but they were, after all, sisters, and sisters had to stick together, or at least that is what Melinda had thought.

In the fall of 1998, things had changed in the Monroe household because the third sister, Mercy Monroe, was born. Normally, it would have been a happy occasion, but their mother, being eighty-four, had passed away during delivery. Oddly enough, the scar on their mother's shoulder, the one that she never spoke of, appeared on their new sister's, just like magic. That was no surprise, though, since the whole family was magic, and weird things happened quite often to them.

Murdock arrived just as the baby was born and scooped her up in his arms. Melinda was overjoyed to see her father. He had never taken much interest in them unless he needed something. Merry Belle, on the other hand, always kept her father at arm's length.

"You are the one little gem; you will be the one to continue the legacy. Now, I must prepare the gifts for the three of you. Melinda, I am entrusting you with the welfare of little Mercy. She is yours until I return. Keep her safe, and you will be greatly rewarded." Melinda took the child and happily agreed to care for the little bundle of joy. Merry Belle rolled her eyes and stayed her distance.

That night, Melinda had fashioned a bassinet beside her bed, and after the baby's nightly feeding, they both fell asleep soundly. Merry Belle had other plans, though, and snuck into her sister's room with a butcher knife ready to slaughter the innocent little child.

Who knows if it was the chimes in the window of Melinda's bedroom or the shine from the metal against the moonlight, but right before Merry dug the blade into Mercy's chest, Melinda awoke and wrestled the knife away from her crazed sister?

"You heard father!" Merry belle screamed, "She will be the end of us all!"

"Where on earth would you get an idea like that?" Melinda said as she wrestled the woman to the floor. Merry Belle knew that she had been bested and stopped the struggle.

"He's going for the sacrifices; as soon as she's old enough, we will be nothing. Dust in the fields."

Melinda looked over at her sister and shook her head again.

"I've noticed a change in you, Merry, ever since that day in the village and with Rigney." Merry glared at her sister with a menacing expression.

"You have no right to say his name. You sealed his fate the moment you chose to have an affair, the moment he chose to betray me. I will never trust anyone again. Not even you." Merry Belle got to her feet and left the room without so much as another word.

Several days passed, and once again, Murdock returned with a nanny and three vials, one for each of them. Melinda drank hers, put Mercy' s in a bottle, and began to feed it to her sister, but Merry Belle wouldn't drink it.

"I know what this is, father, and I won't have it. I accept my fate the way it is; I will not give you my freedom." Murdock smiled and set his case on the table by the door.

"Nanny, would you so kindly finish feeding my daughter in the other room? I have some things to discuss with my middle child." The nanny kept her head down, took the child from Melinda, and went into the kitchen, shutting the door behind her. "You will do as I say, and you will do it with some RESPECT!" Murdock boomed. Melinda was shocked at what she was seeing. Her father had always been kind to them, almost never raising his voice or hands to any of them.

Merry Belle knew that if she didn't do what the man said, he could make her life very horrible; he would do whatever it took to get her to drink the vial, all excluding death, because, if she were to die, his plans would be ruined. Getting to her feet, Merry Belle ran to the cupboard and pulled the same sharp knife out of the drawer, slitting her wrists and falling to the floor, letting the vial roll out of her hand and up against Murdock's shiny black shoe. "My dear, is that all you had left?" He said with a dark laugh. Melinda ran to her sister's side, weeping, covering the wounds with her hands.

"Father, we have to do something. We have to call the doctor." Murdock ignored his oldest daughter's pleas and picked up the vial. Popping the top, he walked over to Merry Belle, who had almost stopped breathing. Her eyes were closed, and her mouth open just enough for Murdock to pour the contents of the little glass tube down the girl's throat.

"There, that wasn't so hard, was it?" He said with a smile. "Never you worry, Melinda, my dear; she will be right as rain in a few hours." Walking over to the door, he grabbed his case on the way out. "You two will always be my family, but we all have to make sacrifices. For what it's worth, you were my favorite. Who knows, you might always be? More than likely, I' m not going to get to spend much time with the new one. Things are moving far too quickly." With that, Murdock left the house, and the sinking realization set in that her sister was correct.

That night, after Merry-belle and the nanny had fallen asleep, Melinda took Mercy into a neighboring town and asked to talk to the local witch doctor. She knew that she couldn't get her sister into the guild's hands herself; her family was wanted for the slaughter of 151 villagers, even though it was Merry Belle who did that all on her own.

"Please, she's my sister, but if we don't do something with her, she could be the death of us all."

"Us all, meaning the Monroes? That doesn't sound like a horrible thing to me." The old man said as he took the baby from Melinda's arms.

"Well then, look at it this way: once my sister is at her best again, she's going to come looking for Mercy and kill her. She's just a baby; how can she defend herself? Can you at least give her a fighting chance?" The witch doctor considered the girl's words for a moment, then nodded.

"What's in it for you?" The old man said.

"Nothing, but I've always thought that family should stick together no matter how messed up things get. I think that when she gets older, we may be able to talk to her, to stop this violence, to stop our father."

"And what if you're wrong?" He said as he swaddled the baby, put her in a carrier, and called to his apprentice.

"Then we die with dignity."

CHAPTER TWENTY-FIVE

Victor had wandered into the old man's bar on more than one occasion, but he never came to get a bite to eat or a stiff drink. No, this man had been here many times since 1998, asking the man about the death of his family and if he knew what had happened.

Few answers had been granted to the poor widow, but still, he returned on the eve of every year. On the anniversary of the day his family passed. Coal always waited for him at the back of the bar, standing between the beaded curtain in a dimly lit back office. Sometimes, Victor had thought people outside could hear them talking, but he quickly knew better. You see, Coal Bearings was a witch doctor, and not just a run-of-the-mill love spell type witch doctor, but the kind that could tell the future and speak to the past, and a lot of people were smart to cross the street when he was out and about.

Coal was less than a charming man, with less than charming ways about him. The only person Victor had seen make the man smile at all was Ann, but she had enough charisma for the lot of them. Usually, the man went to the back of his desk, which was always covered in some creepy trinkets, and sat down as soon as Victor crossed the beaded doorway, telling him whatever he had in the works for someone in town. Tonight was no different.

"Mr. Zanborn, I would ask you what you need, but I'm not losing my marbles just yet. I looked at the calendar; it's that day again. The years keep passing faster and faster these days, probably my old age. Well, let's get to it; I have a vengeance spell to give to Old Mrs. Rucker. Apparently, her husband is sleeping around... Not that I would have the foggiest as to who would want that wrinkly old bag." Victor took a deep breath and sat down in the moldy old green chair on the other side of the desk, lacing his fingers together and waiting for the other part of the ceremony.

Coal always had a set of things he did before reading a person: first, he would give a lecture about why you were bothering him, and then he would take an old Irish corn pipe out of the top drawer and light it ever so slowly. He filled it with some sort of tobacco, but it was none that Victor had ever smelled before, and the smoke let out an eerie gray-blue mist that filled the air with the scent of citrus. That was exactly what he was doing at the moment.

"I need to know if anything has changed, Coal. There have been some developments with the baby." For the first time in years, the old man took his eyes off the wooden match and shook it shut. Putting the pipe on the desk, he leaned in closer.

"The baby, you say. This wouldn't happen to be the Monroe child I sent to you right after you moved here, would it? Would this be a good development or a bad one?" Victor knew he couldn't keep much from the doctor because he had direct connections with Ann, and if he felt so inclined, he could just look into his crystal ball. Victor knew that the ball was just a prop he used to make people feel more comfortable; all Coal really needed to do was touch you.

"I don't really know yet, Coal, you see, the sisters, they must be after her. That can't be good."

"Might not be a terrible thing either, Zanborn." Coal said as he picked up his pipe and lit another match. "In either case, I will keep a close eye on Mercy. She may need guidance." Victor twiddled his thumbs for a moment before speaking up once more.

"There's another thing, as well: the Southpaw lineage wasn't quite as dead as we thought before." Coal put up his hand, indicating he knew.

"Yes, it's quite unfortunate, but not in the way we all thought. I can't go into detail with you now, but I felt her presence the moment she stepped into the meadow." Victor's eyes widened in the realization of what he had heard.

"The meadow?" He said in shock and almost knocked the moldy old chair over, making his way to the doorway, but Coal stopped him in his tracks with his next words.

"I know it's been decades since you got any answers from me that could lead you closer to the answers that you seek, but I believe that it is all going to come out very soon as to who killed your family." Turning around slowly, Victor walked back over to the old man and put two huge hands on the corner of his desk.

"What do you mean, who?" He said, his dark eyes twinkling in the dim light of the room. Coal had lit his pipe and was puffing away at the old thing, blue smoke wafting through the dusty room, making Victor feel quite lightheaded. Bearings put a wrinkled hand over Victor's and closed his eyes, puffing ever so gently on the pipe. He wanted to say something to the old doctor but thought better of it, because tonight might be different from all the other nights, tonight he might get the answers he needed.

"I know I told you that a plague took your babies, that it was orchestrated by someone or something, an event that may happen again. This thing, this someone, is a man of sorts, and he's ripping through the fabric of worlds to find someone... No something. He's coming here, Victor; he's coming for your new family and will stop at nothing to destroy your soul." Victor pulled away from Coal and stepped back a little.

"You don't really believe that it could do that, do you?" Coal opened his eyes and looked at the man; the stress and anger of the chase had aged his face, and the grey mop of hair on the top of his head caused shadows to dance around his deep-set eyes.

"I am not one to judge Zanborn. I have lived a hard life myself and made choices that others may consider evil in my day, but without those choices, I wouldn't be who I am, and I wouldn't be where I need to be to help you now, would I?" Victor's face softened a little as he leaned over once again, looking Coal in the eye. Bearings didn't seem all too concerned about the man's size; the thought of Victor hurting Coal, he knew, never crossed his mind. It was just the sheer frustration that Victor was sorting through.

"I'm a good man, Coal, and I will not make the mistake of crossing that line." Walking to the door, Victor was stopped one last time by the voice of the old doctor.

"We all have choices to make, Victor; no one can judge you unless they have been there." Walking out into the night, he could feel the warm breeze against his washed-out face. The bar always stuck with him for a few blocks: stale cigarette smoke and spilled whiskey, vomit, and the sticky, thick air from bar fights and blood. He always chose to park about three blocks down to clear his head and let the breeze wash away his negative thoughts.

Tonight, though, he felt a little different. Tonight, he could feel the eyes of someone on him. Even though he had chosen to park in an alley, and he knew that the possibility of an old bum or drunkard being around was highly likely, he still couldn't shake the feeling of being watched.

Reaching into his back pocket, he could feel the little hex bag full of morning glories and bluebells. Normally, that would make him less apprehensive, but this did nothing for the man on this night, no, because he knew what was following him wasn't a fairy, and whatever it had meant him no goodness, not even a drop.

"You told me you could protect me!" The voice in the darkness said, in a manic way that put Victor's nerves on edge.

"Who's there?" Victor said as he continued to walk towards his car. He could see it in the distance, just a few hundred yards from where he was, parked under a light post.

"They came to me, Zanborn." The voice seemed to be all around him, walking a little faster; Victor pulled the keys from his coat pocket and pushed the unlock button on his keychain. The voice began to laugh maniacally, and only just then could he hear the footsteps behind him. Turning around, he saw a familiar face right in front of him.

"Richmond?" Victor said with a look of relief and concern. "You look horrible." Richmond smiled and tilted his head to the left and then to the right, almost like a bird would do when it was looking for food. The man began to laugh a little, and Victor's relief began to diminish almost as fast as it had come.

"I look horrible. I look horrible!" Richmond said in a sing-song tone, skipping around the man, who was clearly confused.

"What's going on, Richmond? Why aren't you at your post?" Richmond stopped hopping about and walked right up to the man with a look of rage and despair in his eyes.

"They came for me, the beautiful ones, Victor." Richmond ran his sleeve across his nose, which had begun to bleed. He was pale and sweaty, almost like a junkie looking for his next fix. "They wanted me to give you a message. They want me to tell you to let them in." Richmond's eyes began to twitch as he laughed again, another high-pitched manic sound that echoed through the alley.

"They aren't getting into the guild, Richmond. We put things in place for situations like this. You shouldn't be here; you should have called." Victor pushed past Richmond quickly, who had to jog a little to keep up with the man.

"I... I couldn't; they wouldn't let me. Victor, you have to help me." Victor opened the door to his car and got into the driver's seat, but Richmond quickly slid into the passenger's seat.

"What are you doing?" Victor said, concern turning into anger. Richmond began to laugh nervously and pulled a small gun from his sweatshirt.

"I'm sorry, buddy, but you're going to have to drive now."

"Where are we going?" Victor asked as he slipped the key into the ignition.

"Shadows End, to the publishing company. There's something there that I have to show you."

The drive was a long one, and no matter how much Victor wanted to overpower the tall, thin man, he couldn't for the life of him figure out how he wasn't going to get shot in the process. Every so often, Richmond would let out a little giggle, like there was some inside joke Victor hadn't been let in on, and every mile that passed, the gun-wielding maniac would wipe his bloody nose onto the sleeve of his sweater. It was beginning to look like a bloodbath, and the smell of copper filled the air.

Pulling up to the publishing company, Victor could see that only one light that was still blazing was on the very top of the five-story complex. He could only assume that it was Richmond's office.

"Come on, get out," Richmond said as he got out himself. The passenger side of the car was parked towards the curb, and he stumbled a little. Taking the opportunity, Victor tried to run, but he could hear the gun behind him click and stopped in the middle of the street. "You're pretty fast, but I bet my bullet can outrun you." Richmond giggled as he walked over to Victor and grabbed him by the elbow.

The building was silent and dark; Richmond pulled a flashlight out of his other pocket and handed it to Victor, instructing him to lead the way up the steps to the fifth floor. He knew, at the moment, he didn't have much option and did as he was told. "You know, I never thought I would have the guts to do something like this, Vic. Ha-ha, I mean, who would have thought that mousey old Rich would be kidnapping the head of chapter 151, the nefarious Victor Zanborn." Reaching the door to Richmond's office, Victor could see the light clearly at last from under the crack in the threshold. "Well, don't be afraid, open it," Richmond said as he swayed to the left a little.

Reaching out, Victor turned the knob, not knowing what would be on the other side of the door, but when it swung open, all that they saw was a chair and some rope, and a hanging overhead light that swayed a little from the breeze in the hallway. There was a metal office desk in the corner, a dull shade of tan, and a matching filing cabinet, and that was about it.

"What is this?" Victor asked, but before he had the chance to turn around, Richmond cold-cocked him in the back of the head with the butt of the gun. He didn't know how long he had been out. It could have been minutes, it could have been hours, but the one thing that he did know was that he had been bound to the chair in the middle of the room, and the sound of the crazy man talking to himself had jarred him from his slumber.

"They will be happy, they will!" Richmond said with a giggle. The blood from his nose must have gotten worse because it had spread from his sleeve to the front of his sweater, and the beads of sweat that had formed on the top of his head, well, they were now coming down like small waterfalls covering the top of the man's shirt, copious amounts of moisture. He smelled horrible.

"Please, Richmond, we can talk about this." Victor could feel the warmth of fresh blood on the back of his own head and began to wince at the pain.

"No, no, not now, you are here. They wanted you, and I got you. They will be happy, the WILL!" Richmond began to pace back and forth across the floor, tapping the butt of the gun against his head. "Are you sure you won't let them inside? I did! It's nice." Again, Richmond laughed, but Victor could see the tears in his eyes. He could hear the panic in his voice. He just didn't know how to help.

"I can't; they will kill the girl. They might kill us all. We need to keep our defense up."

"Defense, defense.... DEFENSE!" Richmond began rubbing his face wildly, covering both his palms with his sweater, but it was doing no good. "It's so HOT in here!" He said, as the tears from his eyes stopped and the blood from his tear ducts began.

"What did they do to you?!" Victor said in a panic, trying as hard as he might to free himself from the ropes that bound him in the chair. Richmond put the gun down on the filing cabinet and pulled his sweater off, revealing a long incision from sternum to groin, stitched together with a piece of burlap. It was red and purple, bulging with what Victor thought was an infection. "Oh my God!" Victor began, but that didn't stop Richmond from picking the gun back up.

Pointing it at Victor, he began to cry again, but then stopped as a wave of anger crossed his face.

"You won't let them in, and you won't help me. You couldn't save your family, and you won't save the girl! Your lack of action has consequences, Mr. Zanborn!!" With that, Richmond walked over to the man, pressing the gun to Victor's temple; he cocked the weapon but then quickly pulled it away, stuck it into his own mouth, and pulled the trigger, making the poor man fall backward stumbling across the room and finally lying on his back spread eagle right under the window across from Victor, who was left in shock, his face covered in blood and bound to a chair alone on the fifth floor of a publishing company.

Trying to gather his thoughts, thinking the worst might be over, Victor began to notice the body on the other side of the room and how the cut on the man's chest kept moving, almost as if something on the inside of him were still alive. This time, it was Victor's turn to begin to sweat as his attempts at escape became more panicked. First, the body started to shake, and then it shimmied a little, like a dance to some song no one could hear, and then finally, the protruding gut came open with a mortifying hiss, only to reveal that the poor man's stomach had been gutted and filled with Moon-shadows, and they had taken root inside. Wrapping his spine in vines like a macabre flowerpot. Right before his very eyes, Victor saw the flowers growing, taking over the room and filling the building with a blue, intoxicating mist.

CHAPTER TWENTY-SIX

Misty had barely made it out of the meadows with her life. If the little grey dictator had requested she go in a third time, she would certainly have told him no, but when she had gotten to her feet from the final leap to freedom, Deaththorne was nowhere to be found; in fact, there were signs of a struggle, and Misty could have only imagined what had happened to him.

"Yo, Deaththrone, you out here?" Misty said, her tone was louder than a whisper but not quite a yell. She didn't want to bring attention to herself; more of the rogue fairies might be around any turn. Looking back towards the field, she could see the tall blond woman lying under the tree like an animal, turning in for the night. Misty had seen some things in her lifetime, but that took the cake. What happened at the willow tree, and why do people keep eating that weird fruit it produced? Everyone with a brain knows willow trees don't bear fruit.

She had only made it through the forest a few feet when she saw flashlights in the distance. A large billow of smoke had appeared in the night sky, Misty thought, most likely less than a mile away from where they stood. By the smell of it, more of those monsters were served the same fiery fate as the one she had zapped with the wand she had tucked under her belt.

Hiding in the brush, she could see the lights getting brighter and hear her dog pulling them along the trail, the leash bound tightly to his collar.

"I thought I heard something up ahead." The first man said. Misty saw the flash of silver on his chest and knew they were police officers. Hunching further back into the brush, there was no hiding from the police dog, who began to bark as they got closer to the meadow's edge.

"Hey, you!" The second one said as he pointed the flashlight at Misty, who knew the gig was up. "Come out of there, real slow. Hands where I can see them." Misty put her hands up over her head and made her way out of the brush. The first police officer had his hand on his pistol, ready to fire if needed. "Ma'am, what are you doing out here so late? It's almost three in the morning?"

"Snipe Hunting," Misty said with a sneer as she made her way into the clearing, leaving the bag in the bushes. She had enough on her to explain away without the weird purple flowers getting in the way. Hopefully, they wouldn't look at the most wanted list. If they did, her face would pop right up, and she would be toast. Rolling his eyes, the first officer softened his gaze and relaxed his hand from the gun.

"Come on, Weaver, she's just a kid." Looking over at his partner, he shook his head a little.

"No, Jones, she's not just some kid. She's out here doing something shady." Turning his head back to the girl, who still had her hands up, he took a step closer. Their dog had calmed down but was sniffing the air, probably the smell of dead fairies hurting the poor thing's nose. "Do you know what happened out here tonight?" Weaver asked as he flashed the light directly into Misty's face. She hated cops; they always acted like they were better than you. Flashing their badges and their guns and their flashlights in people's faces. How rude!

"What do you mean, officer?" Misty asked with the sweetest voice she could muster. All she wanted to do was slip away into the night and make her way back to the cabin. Hopefully, Deaththorne was gone. With the wand, she had powers she could have only dreamed of, and getting rid of the fairies would be as easy as a point-and-click.

"Old man Klicken, his corn field was set on fire using an unknown accelerant. The fire department is still trying to get the dang thing out." Weaver began.

"Then there was a fireball that came up from that field over there. Smelled just like the same stuff used to start the first fire. You wouldn't know anything about that, would you?" Jones interjected. Misty cocked her head to the side and smiled her creepy smile. The scar on her cheek crinkled just enough to make her look like her mouth on the right side of her face went all the way up to her ear. Weaver tried not to let the girl see him shiver a little in the warm night air, but her presence suddenly made him uneasy.

"What is it?" Misty asked as she began lowering her hands, taking a step closer to Weaver. She could tell that he was the weaker of the two, and he would be easier to get rid of. The dog that he was holding began to growl as Misty's smile became wider. "Ma'am, I'm going to have to ask you to stop where you are," Jones said as he put his hand back onto his gun. He held the flashlight with the other hand, his fingers twitching with apprehension.

"I'd really rather you call me by my name, Jones," Misty said as she reached behind her, pulling the wand out with a swift motion and pointing it at the man.

"What should I call you then, little girl?" Jones asked, a little less afraid now that she had pulled out a stick and was waving it around.

"The names Misty, Misty Lancaster. Fire!" She screamed, but this time, the wand didn't work; she didn't feel the tingle in her palm, the vibration of power... It was all gone. "I said FIRE!" again, nothing happened, and Misty knew that she had made a grave mistake. She could see the thought process going on the face of Weaver, and then it hit him like a ton of bricks.

"Oh, my GOD!" Letting go of the dog, the man fumbled for his gun, and in the commotion, Misty took the opportunity to run between to the two of them, pulling her tiny lock blade from her sock and clicking it open.

"What the hell are you doing, Weaver??" Jones said as he swung the flashlight behind them, trying to catch a glimpse of the girl who had slipped through their grasp.

"That, that's the girl, the one that killed all those people. She lives in the woods outside of Coral Boy." Weaver was talking over himself and had managed to pull the gun from its holster. "Where did she go?" The police dog began to growl even louder and then bark uncontrollably. The two officers pushed themselves back-to-back, their eyes darting around like crazy.

"Where the hell did she go?" Jones yelled over the barking dog.

"I don't know," Weaver said with a stutter. He had never come face-to-face with a cold-blooded killer before. It was bone-chilling. Weaver had only just made it through the academy last year, but it wasn't for the lack of trying. He had a problem with buckling under pressure; that's why they partnered him with a more seasoned police officer, Jones.

The two of them could hear the girl's laughter in the shadows, but the tall tree and the grass made the sound carry all around them. The police dog immediately stopped barking and began to whimper at the sound and eventually ran off into the meadows.

"Oh great, the damn dog bolted," Weaver said, even though that was the least of his worries at the moment. Misty was crouching low by the tree, and she knew that if she tried to run, the older police officer would spot her. She couldn't risk going to jail. She would be put in the chair for sure. Why might you ask? Because she tried to help the town a little, got rid of the scum that ran the streets, and flooded the river with toxic waste. No, no one would ever understand her, not even the grey ones. She was alone in the world, and sometimes that could be very depressing, but not tonight. Tonight, she got to be the hunter, and the police would be the prey.

"Misty, you have to come out. We will see you if you try to run." Jones said as they began to walk in circles, hoping to catch a sign of the girl.

"Who says I want to run?" Misty called back in a sing-song voice, leaping from her hiding spot and ramming the lock blade deep into Jones' neck. Dropping the flashlight, plunging the three of them into essential darkness, Jones fell to his knees. Pulling at the blade.

"No!" Weaver yelled as he went to his partner's side, "Don't do that! Keep the blade in!" But it was too late; Jones had pulled the knife from his neck. Waves of hot red blood began to spurt from the wound, spraying Weaver in the face and chest. The man tried to use his walkie to call for backup, but the blood shorted out the speaker, and all he could hear was the static of a broken machine. Making his way back to his partner, he pulled the man's head onto his lap, snatching the closest flashlight he had around him. Looking into his friend's eyes, he could see the life force disappear from his body, like a tube television turning off for the last time.

Weaver could feel the emotions welling up inside his throat, and he began to wave the flashlight around with conviction. No, now the girl had made an enemy. Misty had slunk back into the brush, snatching the satchel of flowers up once again. The thrill of the kill still vibrated in her veins. The smile on her face was unaverted by the look of sorrow on Weaver's face. He had gotten to his feet, gun in one hand and light in the other. He was walking ever so deliberately towards the meadows, like he thought he had seen something.

"What the hell is he looking at?" Misty whispered. She was behind him, and if she had another weapon, she would have put the poor man out of his misery.

"Hey, hey you!" Weaver yelled, but Misty could tell what was going to happen next. The tinkling of bells in the distance became louder and louder as one of the Corrowins bombed the man, taking half of his face off. Misty instinctively covered the burns she had gotten earlier in the night, even though they no longer hurt her. Weaver yelled out in pain and then swung over to face Misty, who had begun to climb from the brush.

"I know I said I was snipe hunting earlier," Misty began, "So, Weaver, I would like you to meet the snipe." The man's face was a gnarled mess. It reminded the girl of chewed-up hamburger meat that hadn't yet been cooked. He was missing an eye, and his jawline was exposed, teeth in parts gritted to ashes from the fairy's shark-like attack. She could hear the bells again and knew it was going to advance on him and possibly take his head off.

Weaver twisted back towards the meadows and lifted his gun; as soon as the thing was right on top of him, he shot. The bullet caught the monster in the throat, causing it to bleed all over Weaver's body. Screaming in anguish, the man began to dissolve. His chest caved in, which all but stopped him from making any more noise except for a gurgling sound, and within minutes, Weaver was nothing more than a pile of bloody, back, and red mush in the woods, a mere hundred yards from the meadow.

Misty let out a triumphant hoot as she flung the sack over her shoulder and continued on her way. She had changed her stance on the thought of Deaththorne being dead. Why didn't the wand work anymore? Why did it work at all? What had changed?

Misty stopped in her tracks when she heard the gun cock behind her. She could smell the smoke of old Polk cigarettes and could all but guess who was behind her.

"Saw what you did back there, little missy. Now, why would you want to go and kill that cop for eh?" With a deep sigh, Misty turned around to face Samuel, who had taken a detour when he had heard the commotion, leaving Keen to get Shelby. Even though the man had suffered a pretty severe bite wound, the fairy blood had seemed to seal it shut, making it almost painless, and tonight Keen had used that to his advantage.

"I don't think we've ever met, but I read stories about you when I was little," Misty said with a smile. "Made me want to be a cowboy; I got over it, though."

"Yeah, now it's superhero stuff, right?" Sam said as he took a step closer. The moonlight flooded in, letting Misty get a good look at the man.

"You're a lot younger than I thought you would be."

"I get that a lot," Sam said as he pulled a pair of cuffs from his back pocket. Misty knew better than to fuck with the gunslinger. She wouldn't be fast enough or slick enough to get away. Putting her hands out in front of her, Sam put the cuffs on her and snatched the bag from the little girl. "What were you going to do with this?" He asked, opening the bag and looking inside. "Starshallow flowers?" Misty lifted her shoulders in uninterest and looked off into the distance.

"Thought they were pretty. I was gonna decorate my room with them."

"Hmm," Sam said as he grabbed the cuffs and led the girl toward the meadow.

"You gonna turn me in?" Misty asked, a wave of concern covering her face.

"Not yet," Sam replied.

"Why? I did kill those cops." Misty couldn't get a read on Samuel. There was something about him. Something she thought she liked.

"Last I checked, you only killed the one cop; the other one got the short end of the stick. I'm not gonna send you to the cops right now, little assassin, because you're up to something, and it might have something to do with my friends and a few other people getting into a whole heap of shit. Once this is all over, well, then I can't rightly say. I guess we will see, won't we?" That was the best answer Misty was going to get for the night, and she silently let the cowboy lead her out and around the meadows to the old beater, where Keen Shelby and an old police dog were waiting inside.

CHAPTER TWENTY-SEVEN

Ann had waited for Lark to pass out before she took the red stone necklace and slipped it around her own neck. She knew, for some reason, that the damn thing had made its way into the house. She was relieved, however, that it had stayed in the hands of Lark instead of Shelby, especially after she had vanished to the meadows as she did. With any luck, the men would return shortly, and she would listen to reason.

Looking at the wall clock, she could see that it was pushing three in the morning, and Victor still hadn't made his way home. She didn't want to be an alarmist, but his visits to the doctor were never this long, and she feared that something horrible had happened to him. Looking over at Lark, she could tell that her memories were coming back; Ann hoped that it was the right move. With the Moon-shadow flowers sprouting up all over the property, it would only be a matter of time before they found their way through the magic seal.

Lark had changed drastically from when she had entered. Ann could tell that the woman had grown at least another six inches from the day before. Her shoulder-length, straight red hair had become curly and long, almost to her waist, or at least that is what the Witch had imagined; it had all begun to flow down the sides of the table. Her skin was pale and white, showing the lightest shimmer of blue. Ann thought that it was from the Moon-shadow, but she couldn't be sure whether the color would fade with time or not. She had only heard about the sisters before laying eyes on the baby in 1998, and, of course, the little one hadn't grown into her powers yet.

With the help of the Witch Doctor Coal, Ann had created a memory spell, one that would hide her from her sisters and block her from any visions she would have had invoking her powers to manifest, so, in essence, the two of them stunted her growth, allowing her to become a normal human being, devoid of all magic.

For twenty-three years, they thought that she had lived a normal life, going to college and making friends, but what they didn't rely on or even know about was what had happened the night that Melinda had run away with her sister and the gift that had been given to Mercy. Once she started at the publishing company, they began to notice the things in her books were eerily happening to people all over the world. It would have been easy to pass it off as a coincidence, which was, until she sucked Samuel into a mirror world, one that her mother had remembered as a child, on her journeys with her adopted father, Buck.

Ann and Victor had taken special interest in Lark after Samuel's disappearance and even realized that the girl had a part to play in bringing the old gunslinger back for the second rising. Who knows why Lark's subconscious didn't want Samuel there for the first, but it had to be a good one? Ann was more than shocked when Shelby brought Samuel through the door, and even more so that she was able to hold on to the red stone necklace. Now, Ann feared everyone would be after it. In this realm, it was only one of four stones that could open certain doors, doors to other places, places exactly like the ones we know, but not quite.

There was a quiet knock on the door, and Ann walked over to open it. With any luck, it would be Victor, but her hopes were dashed when her blue eyes landed on Hunter's face.

"How is she doing? It's been an hour." Hunter tried to look over at the girl, but Ann tried her best to block his gaze. Covering the red stone necklace with her shirt, she made eye contact with him.

"Listen, Hunter, she's not going to look the same, not from what you remember."

"What did you do to her?" Hunter said with a glare. Ann didn't have the patience to deal with an unruly, lovesick child at the moment and pushed him out into the hallway, shutting the door behind her.

"It's not so much what I've done to her, Hunter; it's what I've given back." Hunter opened his mouth to speak, but Ann covered it with one of her hands. "It's time you stopped talking and started listening, child. How old are you, twenty-eight? You've seen nothing in this world. You only have a little knowledge of what's out there and the memories and gifts that I'm giving back to Lark; they really weren't mine to take in the first place. What I did, I did so with the best of intentions, but you know what they say about those." She lowered her hand as she could see the pleading in his eyes.

"I want to understand, I really do; I just don't get why she's changing so... so fast." Ann's annoyance turned into sympathy. She could tell that this was no puppy love situation; he could be the one, the one she wrote of in the last book. Ann did have to admit, even though she prophesied, and her words were true, she had a way of drawing you in, making you want to read what she had to say, forcing your eyes to glide over the words like a treat, a dessert for your mind.

Often being alone in the old house, she would take the books off the shelf and read them over and over, pretending to be the female lead of the more adventurous stories, wishing for the day she would have been written about, but as far as she knew, that day had not come. Victor said it might have been because she took the girl's memories and powers that she also took Ann's adventures with them, and she supposed it could be true, because until this day, she had never written about Coal either.

"She's changed, yes, but I didn't take anything away from her, Hunter; when she awakens with any hope at all, she will remember you. She will still feel the same way about you."

"You can't be sure, though." Ann looked over at the man. She wanted more than ever to be the bright light at the end of the tunnel, but she couldn't bring herself to lie to him either.

"I can't tell you that for certain. All we can do is wait and hope."

"Then let me go inside; let me at least hold her hand; it might be the last chance I have to do so." Ann knew the man was right, and if the powers were too much for her to handle, she might be driven to the edge, she might go dark, and she might very well kill her sisters, or worse, kill everyone she ever loved when she was a human. Ann nodded and opened the door. She could feel the red stone necklace against her skin. She had never had one of the stones so close to her before, and she thought she could feel it grow warmer.

Running to the woman's side, Hunter sat down and took her hand. Even though she looked different, he could still see the ghost of the woman he cared for inside her face.

"I'm here now," he said as he stared at the sleeping woman. "I will always be here."

"You know it's a good sign; you woke her from the void. She responds to your voice. She must feel for you similarly, or your voice would have done nothing."

"I do hope you're right, Ann. I don't think my heart would be able to take it if she left me." He could feel his heart breaking a little more at the thought of never being able to kiss her, to listen to her laugh, and watch the twinkle in her eyes as he held her close. He couldn't go back to the life he lived before, not after meeting Lark.

After a few moments, he could feel the grip on the girl's hand begin to tighten, and just as she had fallen asleep, she was wide awake, touching her own face and looking around the room. "Lark?" Hunter asked as he leaned into the woman.

"Hunter?" She said, her eyes an even more vibrant green; at this point, they would have put perfectly cut emeralds to shame. He smiled over at the girl and put his other hand over hers. She smiled down at him, a look of compassion in her eyes. "I can tell you were worried about me, and that warms my heart." Slipping off the table, Hunter helped her get to his feet. He wanted nothing more than to wrap his arms around her, but he thought better of it; she had changed in more than looks, and he could tell.

"How are you feeling?" Ann asked as she walked over to the girl.

"I remember everything, Ann, how you and the doctor took my memories, my powers, and exactly why you did so. I am not angry with you, even though if you had done so with either of my other sisters, you might have become something resembling a walking voodoo doll." Lark smiled, letting go of Hunter's hand, and walked towards the window, looking out into the night. Her words chilled Ann to the core. Her words were honest but cold, not the Lark that she had remembered. Not that she was surprised, either.

"What's wrong?" Hunter asked, following her to the window.

"These powers you gave me, Ann. Can you take them back after we are finished?"

"Finished what?" Ann asked as she met them at the window.

"After I kill my sisters, after Shelby awakens her army. I will need to be put back as I was."

"Why?" Ann asked again.

"Because my father has another gift for me, and I'm not sure if I have these powers, I will be able to resist it. I don't want to be like this." Lark looked down at her new body. She almost towered over Hunter; she had to be over six feet tall, and the power that coursed through her veins was almost too much for her to bear.

"These powers are new. You should have had time to grow into them, but we couldn't risk your sister finding you." Lark looked over at Hunter, putting her hand on his cheek. She smiled ever so kindly and placed a kiss on his other cheek.

"Never you worry, Hunter; even though Lark is gone, Mercy still feels the same love she had deep in her heart for you. She loves you. Hopefully, she can come home." Turning to Ann, her look became more serious, and Ann had to take a step back, worried about what the witch would do. "You, though, have somewhere you had to go. Get your cloak and Andrew. Victor is in trouble." Eyes widening, Ann understood.

"Where is he?" She proclaimed, making her way to the closet and retrieving a dark robe with a thick hood.

"He's at the publishing company on the fifth floor. Ann, he isn't alone."

CHAPTER TWENTY-EIGHT

Coal Bearings wasn't a man of means, not to say he didn't come from a little bit of money. That was what he used to buy the bar he owned and lived in. He had a little apartment that was right above. This little convenience was one of the reasons that he could keep the bar open later than all the others in town.

Right as the clock struck three, Coal put on the last call sign, and in fifteen minutes, the bar was empty, except for the bartender and a waitress who stayed behind to clean up and do some dishes.

"Goodnight. See you tomorrow." The barkeep said to Coal as the old man walked out of his office with a few trinkets and his crystal ball.

"Goodnight, Edward. Make sure that Susan gets to her car safely, and don't stay too long tonight, will ya? Those shot glasses will keep overnight." Edward nodded as he hung the last of the martini glasses in the sky drier and started cleaning the bar itself. Coal never bothered to put a door on his office. He never saw the need. Edward and Susan were like family, and the back of the bar had been sealed with magic. No one who wanted to harm him could walk through the threshold. He had done it to the apartment as well, which made the next series of events especially surprising for the old man.

Getting to the top of the steps, Coal fumbled with his keys. He wasn't too good at juggling things in his hands, so it took him more than one try to get the door open. He thought for a second that he had heard someone or something coming up the stairs behind him, but when he turned around, no one was to be seen.

"Odd," He said to himself, but let the thought leave just as quickly as it had arrived. Getting through the front door, Coal kicked it shut and put his items on the kitchen table. He never left his projects downstairs. In the wrong hands, they could be quite dangerous, not that he thought either of his hires would do such a thing, but curiosity did have a way with people in his experience.

The only thing that Coal had in mind for the evening was sleep. Kicking off his shoes and locking the front door, he made his way through the apartment to his bedroom and laid down on top of the covers. He did this more frequently as the years passed. It was becoming increasingly difficult to stay up as late as he did.

"Maybe I should give Edward that partnership. He does need the money, and I need the rest." That was the last thing the old man said before he drifted off into a dreamless sleep. He couldn't have been down more than an hour when he was jarred from his bed. He didn't know what had awoken him, but as the moments passed, it became painfully obvious.

"Coal, Coal, Coal..." The voice in the darkness began to say, in a tisk tisk type voice. He knew the voice from decades before, but couldn't fathom how she had gotten inside the apartment.

"What do you want, Melinda?" The old mad said. He was lying flat on his back with his hands laced together. He hadn't even thought to open his eyes because he felt safe with the protection spell all around him.

"Why would you lie to Victor like that?" Melinda asked; the question did make Coal open one eye and look down at the foot of the bed. He could make out the woman, her long red hair flowing over her shoulders like a silk waterfall. Her eyes were vibrant and glowing in the dark, like a cat's. Coal could even make out the smirk of a woman who thought she had done something quite clever.

"Again, I ask you what you want, Melinda. You can't do anything to me here. I've forbade it." At the sound of the man's claims, Melinda began to laugh.

"Who exactly do you think you are? Most of your magic tricks are just that... Tricks. My sister and I can break almost anything you throw at us."

"Except for the one thing you want more than anything, right?" Coal said with a smirk. The man refused to move from his bed. He didn't want the witch to think he was frightened, even though he was beginning to become a little bit concerned.

"That one is a little different; you used Ann to help you... Victor won't let us in either, so we're coming to you. We were hoping that we could convince you to..." Coal snorted; Melinda could see his belly in the shadows, moving up and down in a quiet laugh of his own. "What's so funny?" She hissed.

"Do you not think I can see into the future? Yes, it takes me a little while to see... To really see, but what I've witnessed with my own eyes only gives me more conviction. You will never get to Mercy. We won't let you." The look on the witch's face turned from that of amusement to concern and anger.

"Very well," she said, taking a closer step toward the bed. "I convinced my sister to let me come to talk to you alone tonight. I thought I could cater to your better judgment... You do remember what we are capable of, don't you, or have you forgotten?"

"I haven't forgotten what your sister did to those 151 souls that day, but you, you haven't given me a real reason to believe you're like your sister."

"Is that so?" Melinda said with a sneer. She lifted her hand and pointed at the man with a slender finger. Her nails were painted the same color red as her hair, her white gown shifting with her every movement, like two lovers in the night. "I shall take your eyes because you see too much and tell too little."

Coal sat up in pain as he began to feel his eyes burn and sizzle inside his skull. Screaming out in pain, he fell off the bed and onto the floor. Covering his eyes with his hands, he began to whimper a little. The time for bucking up had passed, and he knew that the woman had the upper hand.

"But how, how did you?" Melinda walked over to the man with a look of bloodlust on her face.

"I told you, old man, that your magic isn't any good here, not anymore, and neither are your little trinkets." Melinda leaned down next to Coal's ear because she wanted to make sure that the man heard every single word she was going to say next. "I gave you my sister to keep her safe from Merry, but I told you if the prophecy came to pass, we would die with honor... Correct?" The old man nodded, "Good, then you remember, and the only way that we wouldn't would be not to fight back at all. You and the pink one won't even let us in to see her, let alone fight... What kind of honor is in that?"

"I can't. The spell is done; I can't undo it." Melinda smirked at the cowering man on the floor. Not that he had eyes to see anymore.

"I think next, I will take your lying tongue because you lie to Victor, you hide the truth, and you lie to me." Coal could feel his tongue begin to bubble, and then it popped. Sitting up and coughing blood, the wilted tongue landed on the floor beside Melinda, who picked it up. "Now that the conversation has turned one-sided, I'm going to need you to nod yes or no to the next thing I'm going to ask." Coal nodded yes, even though he was about to pass out from the pain. "Will you let us in? Will you lift the spell?" Coal thought for a moment, for what did he really have to live for?

He had seen, just the other night, what Ann was going to do with Lark's memories. He knew that she was going to need time if she was going to fight the sisters with magic. He also learned another thing, another dark and sinister thing that he didn't dare speak aloud, that was, if he could. He knew what their father had in store for her and that it would take great strength to overcome the trials that were just hours away from happening. Coal thought to himself, What good would come of letting them in? He was old and frail, and Melinda was right; his spells were beginning to lose power. No, he would do one last good thing before she did him in. Nodding no, the old man fell to the floor. He could feel the fire that was his essence begin to flicker a little and thought he had made the right call. More than likely, he wouldn't have made it through the night anyway. Getting to her feet, Melinda screamed. She had done all she could, and now she let the rage inside her consume her better judgment. "I didn't want to do this, Coal; I wanted you, of all the people, to live. When I had no one to turn to, you were there. You saved my sister when she would have surely perished, but now you will not return her when we ask. You are heartless, and so that is the last thing I will take from you. Your heart because you have broken mine."

With a snap of her fingers, Melinda popped Coal's heart, causing his body to seize and then go limp within seconds. A small trickle of blood began to flow from the dead man's ears, and she knew that she had finished what she had come there to do. "It really is a shame," Melinda said as she walked to the front of the house, picking up the crystal ball. "With you out of the picture, we are going to be able to get in, and I'm going to tell Victor everything."

Opening the front door, Melinda let herself out, but hanging by two nails on the other side were two human hearts. One was Edwards and the other Susan's. Two poor sacrifices that broke a spell and killed the third inside.

CHAPTER TWENTY-NINE

Stardock tore through the north side of the meadow. He could see the headlights of the yellow beater on the other side. Bouncing and hiding behind every other tree he came across wasn't doing him any favors with time. He had to, though, because the fairy king was right on his trail and angrier than usual. It wasn't because Stardock was a halfling, even though that was enough to enrage the little troll; tonight, it was because Doc had bested the royal fairy in battle, causing him great discomfort.

Deaththorne wasn't used to being confronted, let alone injured in battle. If he had been at full power, if he had his queen by his side, Stardock wouldn't have stood a chance. Deaththorne knew, though, that if he could just get his hands on the little man, he could take him down once and for all, but he was quick and an expert hider.

"Come out here!" Deaththorne yelled into the night, causing the whooping cranes to fly out from the high brush in front of him. Stardock took the opportunity to leap across a small divot in the ground, rolling onto his back and lying perfectly still in the brush. He knew his only hope was to reach the car before they drove away. They wouldn't leave him... Would they?

Deaththorne stomped through the woods, knocking down thorn patches and using his claws to rip down brush and bushes in his path. Letting out a roar, the sound echoed through the land like an angry bear. "Come out!" The longer it took for the fairy to find his prey, the more furious and more erratic he became, almost delirious with madness.

Turning his back to the halfling once again, Stardock took the opportunity and got to his feet, sprinting around the meadow. He could hear the bad belt start and the engine rev, but he was still too far away from it to be seen.

"No," He whispered as he held a hand out into the night, but this time, his movements didn't work out in his favor, and the fairy king tackled Doc, causing them both to fall into a thicket of briars.

"You think you can attack me and just get away with it?" The king fumed as he rolled Stardock onto his back. Deaththrone's rage both amused and frightened Stardock. Instinctively, the little man covered his face with his hands as the troll jumped up and landed squarely on his chest with a thud. All the air left the poor halfling's lungs, and he did all he could from passing out.

Deaththorne had a large gash across his face from the attack, and Doc could hardly believe he had had the bravery to do so. As soon as Shelby had lifted the meadows' poison and allowed the fairies to enter, Deaththorne was at the ready, but Stardock wouldn't allow him to enter. Something in the back of his mind told the little fellow that Deaththorne might know about the second tablet, the one that only Stardock and Coal knew about... The one that tells the REAL truth about the second resurgence.

Leaping into action, Stardock had retracted his own set of talons and ran them across the King's face, slicing his grey skin like butter with a hot knife, hence the chase and now the inevitable demise of the small soldier.

"Don't forget to tell them who gave you that beauty mark," Stardock said with a little laugh. A small trickle of blood began to form at the corner of his mouth. He could hear the car in the distance as it began to drive off into the night, and Stardock knew that they had, in fact, left him for dead.

"I would, old man, but I doubt they would believe me or even care." Stardock's eyes shut as

Deaththorne put a jagged hand around the halfling's neck, tightening his grip ever so slightly. He wanted to make Doc's death painful and slow.

"My friends would, they would believe.." Stardock put his hands around the King's and tried to free himself from his grasp, but it was no use. Letting out a large laugh, the King took his other hand, pointing his index finger up into the air, and then pressed it against Stardock's chest.

"You have no friends; you're an abomination, a freak!" Pushing his long black talon down onto the little one's chest, he began to pierce Doc's flesh. Letting out a cry of pain and sadness, the creature closed his eyes, letting a little tear roll down his face. This thrilled the fairy more than words could describe. Pushing down harder, he began to choke Stardock, watching him squirm and flail under his strength.

"I wouldn't be so sure about that." A voice called out from behind the two fairies; Deaththorne smiled and looked over at Doc for the last time.

"Fresh meat!" Thorne's smile became wider and wider as he dislodged his jaw like a snake, ready to consume Stardock headfirst with one big gulp, but didn't have the chance when Drew ran at the fat little monster and punted him across the brush, causing the embedded talon to fly out of Stardock's chest, ripping his flesh just a bit. Leaning over, Drew helped the halfling to his feet and rushed them back through the north side of the meadow.

"What are you doing here?" Doc asked, even though he was grateful for the save.

"We don't let our friends down, and you're a friend. Always have been." Doc looked over at Drew and nodded. He had to hold back tears; this was no time to get sappy, but he had thought, even if it were just for a second, he could have been forgotten so easily.

"We need to go. Deaththorne is going to be even more enraged. He has just one more night before the door becomes useless." Stardock said, looking ahead.

"Well then, we'd better speed it up," Drew answered with a smile. They both could see Ann at the top of the ridge waiting for them. Her hooded cloak would come in handy if they were out after the sun rose.

"Ann can get us where we need to go, and that's to Shadows End."

"Why?" Stardock asked.

"Victor, something happened to him; he never returned. Mercy told us where to find him, but he wouldn't be alone." Reaching Ann, she nodded to the two of them and pulled The Mother's Heart out from under her cloak. Slicing her hand and placing it onto the stone, she motioned for them to come closer.

"Imagine the publishing company; imagine where you want us to be." Stardock could smell her fresh blood, and he could barely contain his lust for it. Hunger rushed over him. Closing his eyes, he thought of the publishing company, full of people... Delicious warm people.

CHAPTER THIRTY

"How did you get those roots out of her?" Misty asked as she looked over at the big goon sitting in the back seat beside her. Samuel thought that it would be best if Keen sat in the back so he could let his leg heal up a little on the way back to the cabin, but Misty was a chatterbox, asking a bunch of dumb questions.

"What in tarnation are you on about now, little one?" Samuel couldn't help but notice the nothing look on Keen's face and the way that the color had rushed from his skin. He could see small beads of sweat begin to roll down his forehead and feared that it might be the start of an infection. Hell, Samuel knew that those things didn't have a great dental plan. Their jagged teeth are always yellow and protruding like a shark's.

"The roots. That blond girl, she was all like, 'I'm the Qhizyja, blah blah blah.'" Misty held her cuffed hands out in front of her as she spoke, wobbling her body back and forth like an old-school zombie. Putting her hands down again, she looked over at Keen. He hadn't said much since they had gotten into the car, and to be frank, the lumberjack put her off a bit. "What's wrong with big, tall, and sweaty over here?" Letting out a little sigh, Samuel rolled his eyes. It had been a while since he had to deal with a teenager, and it was already starting to wear on his patience.

"Don't you mind him none either, alright? He got bit by one of those little fairy friends of yours. Probably caught a virus or something."

"Awe, snap!" Misty said with a smile, her large brown eyes twinkling in the moonlight, a mischievous glow in them. "Ya know what happened to that girl up on the mountain, ya know the one."

"Yeah, I figured you would know about the sisters. They were made of magic, though; Keen, well, he's just a man, plain and simple."

"You know you don't believe that," Misty said with a sneer. "Let me take the old guy out. It would probably be better for him in the long run." Samuel made the next turn a little sharper than he needed to, sliding around the stop sign and passing the firetrucks that had finally put out the flames in the cornfield. Sam thought he saw the strange little man again, waving on the opposite side of the road, but he couldn't have been certain. The old police dog slid across the front seat and bounced up against Shelby, who was fast asleep against the door.

"Listen here, little assassin, you will do no such thing. You got that!" Misty nodded at Sam, who had slowed the car down; they had almost made it back into town, and that made Samuel feel a little better.

"But for real, though, how did he get the roots out of her? Her eyes were all glowie, and she was saying weird shit; a friggin' wand popped out of her wrist. Samuel... a WAND! How does that crap happen?" Sam looked into the rearview mirror. He could see the girl steadily eyeballing Keen, but he had no reason to believe she would be lying to him.

As they were passing the hotel on Dodson, they were stopped at a light; Samuel took the opportunity to look down at the girl's bare feet. She had tucked them under herself as she slept, but it was more than obvious that there were wounds. They didn't look horrible, but they were there, nonetheless. He also began to notice the holes in Shelby's pants as well.

"What the..." The man was cut off by the sound of a honking car behind him and looked up to see that the light had turned green.

"See," Misty said, "I told ya.' You got some seriously fucked up friends, cowboy, and if you think I'm the bad guy, so that you know, your little blond friend tried to fry my ass like bacon in the meadows. She's a killer, too; I can smell my own." Misty didn't realize it at first, but the holes in her arm had begun to itch, and she had begun to pick at them. Looking down distinctively, she could tell that something was up.

"You good back there?" Sam asked as he took another look in the rearview, but this time, Misty's attention wasn't on Keen. She was looking down at something, but Samuel couldn't quite tell what. Pulling up to the bottom of the driveway, Samuel typed in the code, and the four of them made their way through the gate and up the mountain.

"I always wondered what was up here. Heard some fun stuff about this place. Would have loved to have been part of that action." Sam couldn't help but roll his eyes again at the girl. He thought if she weren't such a raging homicidal maniac, they would have gotten along.

Pulling to the front of the cabin, Keen finally did something by grabbing onto the girl's cuff and leading her out of the car. Misty wanted to say something, but now wasn't the time or the place for her wit. Something wasn't quite right with the man, and even though Samuel wanted everyone to think he was just delirious with fever, Misty knew better. She knew the stories of Sir Greaty and Faith. Would he, too, start killing wild hogs? Would he smash the heads in of all that got in his way? Misty sure hoped so.

Sam got out of the car and picked Shelby up. The dog jumped out on his own and made his way around the back of the house. Samuel figured the drive had made him have to go to the bathroom, so he left it be. Opening the front door, the three of them walked into the foyer. Misty had never seen anything this size before, and it was a little much for her to take in.

"Wow, this place is massive. Got anything to eat?" Misty asked. She wanted to wander the grounds, but Keen still had a tight grip on the girl's cuffs. She was really beginning to dislike being so close to the man, whose sweating had become more labored within the last twenty minutes. Samuel made his way up the steps with Shelby, who hadn't so much as moved. He thought she must have been extremely tired, and why shouldn't she be? The woman had gone almost forty-eight hours without lying in a bed. As he disappeared up, another face began its descent down.

Hunter couldn't sleep, not with all that had gone on a few hours before. Every so often, he could feel a wave of sleep wash over him, making him slightly lightheaded, but his friends were out there, and he wanted to make sure they returned safely. Lark had retired to her room, most likely to get some rest of her own. He hadn't heard a peep out of her since then and was far too uncertain about their future to risk knocking on that door just yet.

"Keen, what happened to you?" Hunter asked as he took the girl in the cuffs away from the man. Fishing around in his pocket, Keen handed Hunter the keys to her prison and nodded.

"Lock her down," Keen responded breathlessly and then stumbled back a few feet. Hunter knew that he didn't have a lot of time to waste, so he pulled the girl along like a dog on a leash up the steps and into the far back bedroom, the only one that hadn't been occupied and the one that Hunter didn't want to go into.

Misty thought she could wrestle away from Hunter, but getting past the other two would be another story completely, so she played along and allowed the man to cuff her to the bedrail.

"Geez, aren't ya gonna buy me dinner first?" Misty said with a laugh, but Hunter didn't find it funny; in fact, in this room, nothing was funny. He could still remember Hannah like it was yesterday, the way that she picked William up and threw him around like a rag doll, how she had three men at her mercy, how something so powerful could be destroyed, but the destruction of something so delicate.

"Pardon me if I don't stick around to chat, but I have a friend to look after," Hunter said without bothering to turn around. He wasn't sure what the girl had done to get locked down, but if Keen said she needed to be, then she did, and at this point in the game, Hunter wasn't going to take any chances.

Turning off the light and shutting the door, Hunter made his way down the hall and descended the steps once again. He found Keen sitting at the dining room table. He had pulled a chair back and propped his injured leg on it to try to ease the throbbing.

"It stopped... Hurting, but now it's come back." Keen said as he pulled the leg of his government-issued black pants up to expose the wound. Hunter's mouth opened a little in shock as he began to realize the severity of Keen's injury.

"Oh, my... Let me get a first aid kit." Hunter said as he wandered out of the room and into the downstairs bathroom. Sure enough, under the sink was a simple kit, but that was all he needed for now. Running back to his friend, he opened the box and pulled out a pair of gloves, popping the top off the cleaning agent. He screwed on the squirt tip and began to spray it onto the wound. Keen winced but allowed Hunter to keep cleaning the area.

"Can you tell me how this happened?" Hunter asked as he took a pair of tweezers from the kit, peeling back pieces of necrotized flesh.

"I got bit by a fairy... Then it bled on me." Nodding, Hunter continued to look at the wound. Something was protruding from the edge. Something odd, Squinting Hunter tried to get a better look, but couldn't.

"I'm going to have to extract a piece of foreign matter from your wound. I'm not going to lie. It's going to hurt, but if I don't, the outcome might be much worse." Keen nodded and motioned for him to continue.

Taking the tweezers, Hunter pinched down as hard as he could, pulling the yellow jagged thing from Keen's open wound. The man began to yell in pain, but after a few seconds, the object was out and on the table.

"A tooth?" Keen said as he looked down. Hunter nodded in wonderment.

"It must have gotten lodged in your femur. Who says you can't take it with you?" Hunter said, smiling at the man. "In any case, it looks like you're in the beginning stages of Carbuncles on the outer layer around the bite. On the inside, I'm afraid I don't know what I'm looking at. Necrotizing Fasciitis would have been my first guess, but after I peeled the black goo off of your wound and washed it... Well, it looks alright." Hunter could tell that his diagnosis couldn't have been 100% correct. Keen's face was pale, and he was sweaty, more than likely burning up with fever, but he had no more answers to give, at least not without lab work.

Pulling some aspirin out of the box, he handed them to Keen. "Let me look for a sewing kit. We will get you sewn up, and then you can get some rest. Tomorrow, I will get you to the hospital for medication."

CHAPTER THIRTY-ONE

Ann, Drew, and Doc all walked up to the publishing company. Victor's car was parked outside, against the curb.

"The door's unlocked," Stardock said as he pulled the door open and peered inside.

"That's… Convenient." Drew muttered as he walked over towards his friend. "Be careful, remember what Mercy said; he's not alone in there."

"Not only that." Ann responded, "We don't know what things are up there either." The boys nodded at Ann as they made their way into the building. They saw from the outside that the fifth floor had a light shining, like a beacon.

"He has to be at the top, right?" Stardock said. He was leading the way, due to the fact that the little man could see in the dark much better than the other two could.

"I would assume so," Drew responded. He had pulled a small penlight out from his front pocket, but it did little good to illuminate the staircase in front of them. Ann was quiet, following the sounds of their footsteps. She was all but blind in the night, but didn't want them to fuss over her. She was far too proud, and she didn't want them to take their mind off the mission. Victor had been stuck here for god knows how long, and he could be injured... Or worse. Stardock stopped in his tracks as he heard something a few floors down.

"What was that?" He said with a little whimper. Andrew put a comforting hand on the little halfling's shoulder.

"Let's just keep going, you've got this, Doc." Shaking his head, the little man continued up the stairs; they had made it to the fourth floor when Ann heard the sound again.

"Guy's, that's not nothing... That certainly is something." Looking up at the two dark figures of her friends, her eyes widened.

"We need to go... NOW!" The three of them sprinted up the stairs as they began to feel the scurry of little feet running past them.

"What the hell!??!" Drew said as he began to kick the rats out of his way. They began to claw at his ankles and bite into the soles of his shoes. "What do they want?" Andrew yelled.

"The witches are controlling them!" Ann yelled from behind. She couldn't stand the vermin. The smell of plague and death followed them, and that made her skin crawl.

"They're delicious," Stardock muttered as he put one after another into his open mouth. He hadn't realized how hungry he had actually become until just now, and with every mouse he consumed, he could feel his strength begin to return.

"Eww," Drew said, taking his hand off the halfling. Making it to the top of the steps, the three of them ran to the door. They could see blue mist and a faint light casting an eerie glow from under the threshold.

"Over there." Stardock pointed, putting one final rat inside his mouth. The crunch of its tiny bones echoed through the empty hallway. Ann couldn't wait to get out of the hallway and haphazardly pushed past the two men.

"No, wait!" Drew said, but it was too late. Ann had flung the door open, casting the hallway in eerie blue mist. For some reason, the rats retreated down the stairs and into the darkness.

"What's that smell?" Doc asked, but Drew knew immediately that something was wrong with the little man. His eyes were unblinking, and his little body began to sway as the blue fog encompassed the hallway.

"Moon shadows, I should have known," Ann said under her breath. Drew began to feel a little out of it himself, but managed to get to the doorway before he needed help standing. Propping himself against the doorway, Andrew began to shake his head. He could feel his brain jiggling around like a marble in a cup.

"Why do I feel like this?" He asked as he looked over at Ann, but now his vision was beginning to blur as well, and he thought he could see two women beside him. Charging into the room, Ann ran to the window and opened it, picking up what Drew thought to be a giant flowerpot, and attempted to heave it out of the window. It proved to be more difficult than Ann had originally thought because the vines from the flowers had begun to climb the walls beside the dead man's body.

"It's always something," Ann muttered to herself and began to harness the powers of the fairies. Her skin started to turn grey, and thick, black talons formed at the end of her long, slender fingers.

"What's going on in there?" Drew asked drunkenly. "Is that large lump over there, Victor?" He pointed to the limp man in the chair, but couldn't get it together long enough to let go of the door frame.

Slicing at the vines, Ann managed to free the corpse from the wall and pick him up, using her newfound strength. Within moments of throwing him five stories down and watching him splat to bits on the pavement, the blue mist began to dissipate, and Andrew's wits began to come back to him.

Once he thought he could walk a straight line again, Andrew entered the room and began to help Ann untie Victor, who was still unconscious.

"A little help, Doc?" Drew yelled from the room, but there was no answer. "Doc?"

"I fear the halfling has inhaled too much of the Moon-shadow mist. We have to get him back to the cabin soon, or he may stay that way." Ann began, but the sound of a woman at the entrance of the room laughing made them both stop in their tracks.

"I can't believe that's all I had to do to get you here... Just take your fearless leader. You walked right into our trap, and I've already put one of your little friends here to sleep. Don't worry, he's in Lala land where he belongs, probably dreaming of chasing cars or something."

"He's a halfling, not a dog!" Drew hissed as he got to his feet. He could hear Victor behind him moaning and knew it wouldn't be too long before the man would come around. Ann stayed crouched behind the chair, clawing with her talons at the rope. The woman in the doorway was tall and beautiful, with mesmerizing eyes. The kind that would suck you in and spit you out. Her skin was flawless and porcelain, and the white Roman-style dress she wore danced with delight whenever she moved even an inch. Andrew couldn't keep her eyes off the girl. He knew he shouldn't look, but he couldn't help himself.

"Andrew, you can't look at her!" Ann said as she let the ropes fall to the office floor and got to her feet. "Why don't you try that on me, Merry Belle? I bet you won't be so successful."

"I don't need to be." Merry Belle said as she walked into the room. All of a sudden, Ann felt a pain in her heart, one she had never felt before. "You see, my sister paid your friend on the south side a little visit. She should be on her way here now."

"Coal," Ann said with a hint of sadness and panic in her voice. "What did you do?" The witch laughed and walked into the room.

"Smart of you to throw out the old body. I was hoping it would take you a little longer than it did, but I can make do with this as well." Ann lifted her talons, ready to advance on the girl, but Merry just lifted her hand and waved Ann across the room. Andrew couldn't do a single thing. His eyes couldn't be torn from the woman's immense beauty. Her hair fell down her back like a wave of magic, her lips as red as a rose, what he would give for a single smile from her beautiful face. Yes, the man had become completely entranced.

Victor began to stir from his slumber when he heard Ann hit the wall beside the old tan filing cabinet.

"What, what happened?" Victor began. His vision was still blurry, and he couldn't see much of anything at the moment, which worked in Ann's favor.

"The woman in white! She's one of the witches; she must be stopped!" Getting to his feet, Victor attempted to charge at the woman, but his legs were still shaky, and he stumbled short, falling to the floor in the middle of the room. Again, Merry laughed. Even louder this time because the woman knew that she had won.

"You know, I think I will take a trinket or two myself. Why should Melinda have all the fun tonight? Or should I say this morning?" Ann looked over at the window and saw the sun begin to rise in the east. Oh, why did this corner office have to be on the east side of the building? Merry Belle walked over to Ann and leaned over her, but the woman was distracted by the ray of light that had begun to descend across the room towards the open door and soon flooded the hallway where the halfling lay unconscious.

Ann tried to get to her feet, but the witch used one of her hands to hold her down.

"I'm not finished with you yet, Ann. How is it that something as strong as you, something as bright as you, something as beautiful as you can't tell yourself who or what you are? Can't you see? Ann, what it is you are?" Victor tried to get to his feet again, but a wave of dizziness washed over him. How long had he been out? He had to think of something and fast. "I think I will take one of your eyes, beautiful and blue, just like the sky on a perfect day, because you can't see your own worth." Without so much as another word, Ann began to feel her eye begin to bulge and swell inside of her head. Putting one grey hand over her face, she let out a scream of pain that rang through the company walls, shaking the windows and causing them to crack in their seals.

Getting to his wobbly feet, Victor looked over at Drew, who was staring, unblinking, at the witch who only looked like a red and white blob to Victor. He had to knock him out of it. Stumbling forward, the large, mammoth man tackled the much smaller man to the ground, causing him to hit the back of his head hard against the floor.

Andrew began to see stars, but the witch's vision had left his mind.

"Oh my god, Ann!" Drew said as he tried to get to his feet, but Victor held him down for a second.

"Don't even look that way. You need to help Doc, and you need to do it now!" Taking off his coat, he handed it to Andrew. Looking over, Drew could see the light from the sunrise begin to engulf the whole room and creep out into the hall. Scrambling to his feet and taking the large coat with him, Drew ran to the hall, throwing the coat on top of Stardock like a blanket, and then, for good measure, he shut the door behind him, leaving the three alone in the room.

"What did you do?" Ann screamed in pain and rage as she tried to get to her feet, but for some reason, the woman's single hand kept her on the floor, pressed against the depressing tan wall.

"You have brought it to me on a pretty pink platter." Merry Belle said, smiling as she reached her free hand out, ripping the Mother's Heart from around Ann's neck. She could feel the hate boil up inside her, her pink tone turning a darker shade, almost fuchsia, and then the woman smiled.

"You know, you're right about one thing. I am powerful, and I should know what I am." Ann said. Merry Belle sneered as she looked over at the blood-covered stone in her hand.

"That you should." It was Merry's turn to be entranced by something. She could see the reflection of her face in the perfectly cut gem, and it was a sight to behold. Lifting one of her hands, she opened her talons, long, black, and deadly, slipping them through the witch's throat. Stumbling back in shock, Merry Belle fell to the floor on her back as Ann got to her feet.

"I know what I am, Merry; I know exactly what I am." The witch began to open her mouth to speak, but nothing came out. Gurgles of blood formed around the corners of her nose. She began to push herself back, but was stopped by a large foot. It pushed down onto her shoulder, and she looked up to see Victor, who had his eyes squarely on Ann. Her smile said everything as she lifted the bloody talons over her head once again. "I will tell you right now, Merry Belle, I am the one thing you hate, the one thing that will bring you and your sister down. I am a WARRIOR!" Bringing the talons down hard, Ann thought she would have sealed the witch's fate, but all she got back were fibers from the carpet she sliced to bits. The witch had vanished, and with it, the red stone.

"Oh no, no, no, no," Ann said as she began to grab her neck in a panic. Her talons began to vanish, her pink skin returning to her arms, but the eye that had been stolen did not return, and all that was left was an empty hole, almost as if it had been cauterized.

"What? What happened, Ann?" Victor said as he began to stumble backward again. The woman was able to catch him this time and lead him back to the chair he had been bound in.

"I will tell you, but you're not going to like it." Victor rubbed his head as the sun had finally risen to meet the morning sky.

"Just tell me." He muttered.

"Alright," Ann began, taking a step back, "She's got the stone."

CHAPTER THIRTY-TWO

The sun had begun to rise over the cabin, and everyone had drifted off to sleep, even Hunter, who had passed out in the hallway with his back propped up against the wall beside Lark's shut bedroom door. He was jarred awake when he began to hear the door to the room open a little, and a meek voice call out to him.

"Hunter?" Scrambling to his feet, he turned to face the girl who had opened the door just a crack. Her shoulder-length red hair was in a knotted mess. He could see her slender frame pressed against the threshold, and a smile crossed his lips.

"Lark?" She nodded as she cracked the door open a little more and took his hand.

"I don't know where she went, Hunter, and I don't know how much time we really have together; all I do know is that I'm grateful that you are here with me right now." Taking a step closer to the woman, he could feel his heart racing. He didn't think he would have the chance to lay eyes on her in this form again. Pulling him into the room, they embraced for a long moment. The white Roman-style dress that she had been wearing the night before, two sizes too big, hung on her like a tent. "I need to tell you something, Hunter, before I go." Hunter pulled himself away from her, looking into her large green eyes. He could see the sadness, and he thought his heart would shatter into a thousand pieces. He wanted more than anything to take away the hurt.

"You can tell me anything." He whispered. She pulled him in close once again and placed her head on his chest, listening to the sound of his rhythmic heart. She knew that it beat solely for her, and it brought her comfort.

"You have to let me go, Hunter; I can't ask you to live this life with me. I want you to be happy." Hunter could feel the sadness building in his chest. The lump in his throat began to swell; he knew he was going to cry. Swallowing hard, he put a hand on the back of her head, caressing her silky red hair.

"You know if you asked me to do just about anything, I would with no questions asked, but I will not... No, I cannot do this thing that you're asking me to do now. There is no one in the world out there for me but you. I would walk through space and time to find you again." And in that moment, Hunter understood what it was like to be hopelessly humbled and renewed by untainted and pure love. Oh, what William must have gone through when Darla slipped through his fingers not once but twice, and he still chose to fight beside his friends.

"I don't know if I will be able to fight my way back when Mercy returns. I know she will; she has a mission. She's strong, Hunter. Stronger than I am. I don't want you to leave my side... I want to be with you." Lark pulled away from Hunter, letting her dress fall to the floor and pushing the door shut with her bare foot.

CHAPTER THIRTY-THREE

Down the hall, Misty had fallen asleep on her back. Small rays of sunlight began to peek through the sheer curtains on the window beside the bed. It had been a long time since she had slept anywhere other than her cot, and it showed. As the sun rose higher in the sky, its beams filled the room, bathing Misty in the glow of the morning.

Jumping up with a start, the girl looked over at her arm. It had begun to smoke in the sun.

"What the hell?" She said to herself as she took in the rest of what the morning had to offer. Her naturally tan skin had begun to take on the color of the fairies, just on the infected arm, or so she thought. On the end of her fingers were the beginnings of black, razor-sharp talons. Pulling on her infected arm, she was able to escape her cuffs easily. Jumping from the bed, she made her way to the door. Noticing that the smoke had begun to go away. "Must be the infection. I'm not immune to the sunlight anymore. That's a bummer." She said to herself as she opened the door and ventured out into the hallway.

Everyone else had to be asleep because the house was as quiet as a tomb, and the only thing she could think about was food. Her stomach was growling. She was certain there would be a kitchen on the bottom floor, so she began venturing there. As she made her way down the steps, she passed a small wall mirror and had to stop to take in the shocking sight of her own face.

The left side still looked like her, with the scar and the wild, wide brown doe-like eye, but the right side was someone entirely different. On the right side, she donned a new one, a large black marble of an eye, set inside the now slightly greyish skull of the girl. She thought her mouth looked normal, but for some reason, there was a small slit that went from the corner of her mouth to her ear, and when she opened it, her jaw unhinged to show a set of gnarly shark-like teeth. "Wow..." She hissed, "I'm even more badass than I was yesterday."

Making her way to the bottom floor, the girl began to sniff the air. She could smell something on the other side of the wall, or was that someone? The smell was all too familiar, but what was it? Paying it no mind, Misty snatched an old coat from the rack at the bottom of the stairs in the foyer and wrapped it around herself to block the sunlight as she wandered about, looking for the kitchen.

Walking through the dining room, someone had left the cuff keys, an open first-aid kit, and bloody gauze on the table; the girl wandered around the corner.

"Bingo!" she said, rubbing her hands together. Running to the refrigerator, she swung the door open and began to pull things out one by one. First, she tried a fruit tray, but something was off about it. When she took the first bite, all she could taste was rot. Spitting it out onto the floor, she ran to the sink and gulped water straight from the tap.

"Ugh, someone has to clean out that fridge." She muttered as she made her way to the next shelf. There, she found some leftover cake, but again, all she could taste was decay. "What the fuck!" She hissed as she threw the cake on the floor. The last thing she tried before giving up completely was a box of fried chicken. It, too, was horrible, almost as if whoever cooked it burned it to death with propane.

Walking out of the kitchen, feeling discouraged, she passed the dining room table and began to smell that intoxicating aroma again. What was that? Her mouth began to water as she looked down at the blood-soaked bandages on the table. "Ah, hell no..." She whispered, but it was already too late to fight back. Her fairy instincts were too strong. Snatching the gauze from the table, Misty stuck them in her mouth and began to suck the blood from them like a vampire. The rush she felt when it touched her tongue was amazing, and all she wanted to do was get her hands on more. She was almost too distracted to hear the sound of the front door opening, but came back to reality when she heard the voice of a man in the foyer.

"Quick!" He said, "Get Doc to the observation room! Ann, you have to go with them. God knows what that witch did to your eye."

"Did he say witch?" Misty whispered to no one in particular. Pulling the bandages out of her mouth, Misty slid under the dining room table and waited for the people in the foyer to vanish down the hall and into another room. Now, she thought to herself. Where could she get some fresh blood?

Upstairs on the second floor, Keen had fallen into a deep sleep. His wound hadn't gotten any better because of it; no, in fact, he could feel the infection spreading through his leg. What had the bite done to him? He fought to wake up, but he was stuck in his nightmarish dream, one where he was bound to help the people he came here to stop.

He was walking in the forest at night with what could only be described as a goblin. It had one black beady eye and a clawed hand. As disgusted as he was by the thing, though, he was bound to her by some force. Something bigger than himself, something he didn't know how to fight. The feverish sweats made him shake, but he couldn't move. He was unable to pull the covers over himself.

Slipping into his room and closing the door as quietly as she could, Misty slithered over to the sleeping man's bed. The smell of his blood was in her nose now, and she had a taste for it. Taking one of her black nails, she cut away at the man's shirt sleeve, revealing his strong arm. Misty licked her lips. She couldn't wait to feast on his blood. Opening her snake-like mouth, she bit down ever so gently, causing a handful of superficial cuts just deep enough to cause the blood to drip from the man's arm.

Keen groaned a little from the pain but was unable to wake himself. She drank her fill, and only then did the lumbering man awaken. Misty jumped back with a start, but he did not attempt to pursue her. She tilted her head in confusion.

"You're not gonna hurt me?" she asked as she got to her feet. Keen, now sitting up in his bed, looked over at his arm. It had stopped bleeding, but he knew what she had done. Inside his mind, he wanted to take the girl down. To arrest her and put her away, but his body wouldn't let him.

"No," He said groggily. Getting to his feet, he looked around the room for his shoes. "We go now." He said again. He wasn't even looking at Misty, but she was amused at the thought of having her own bodyguard and allowed him to wander about.

"Where are we going?" She asked. But the man just kept walking in circles.

"We go now." Flopping back onto the bed, he picked up his shoes and looked at them like they were foreign objects. The girl sighed and walked over to the man. She had never felt obligated to help anyone before, but today felt a little different. Maybe it was because they had shared experiences with the fairies, perhaps it was because he tasted so good to Misty, and having a snack on the road would be a lot more fun than not... Or maybe it was because she was lonely. In any case, she knelt and took the shoes from Keen's hand.

"I will help you." She said as she slipped the shoes onto the man's large feet. She could see the wound on his ankle and that someone had attempted to patch him up. It was good work, she should know; she's stitched herself up a time or two before herself. "Now, where are we going? The sun's out, and it burns my skin. It might hurt you, too, you big oaf." Keen tilted his head to the side. She wasn't sure if he understood, but then he got to his feet and disappeared into the bathroom, shutting the door behind him.

She could see the lights turn off and then on again. At first, she thought he was stuck in a loop like before, but then the door opened, and he walked out with a bottle of sunblock. Misty snorted a little but took the bottle from his hand.

"What do you want me to do with this?" She asked as she looked over the bottle.

"Put on. Helps. We go now." She gave the large man an odd look but did as she was told. It couldn't hurt to try. Opening the shutters on the side window, Misty stuck her hand out into the sun. It tingled a little, but nothing she couldn't handle.

"Well, shit, Igor, it really fuckin' works. Thanks." Looking out across the lawn, she began to understand what the man meant about leaving the cabin. Misty could see the sisters walking from the mountain's ledge, and they didn't look happy.

"We go now," Keen said as he walked towards the bedroom door. Shutting the window, Misty took Keen's hand, slipping the sunblock into her pocket.

"Yeah, ya' big brute, we go now."

CHAPTER THIRTY-FOUR

Shelby woke from her slumber. She couldn't remember a thing from the night before, but she could feel sharp pains in her legs, like little thorns trying to make their way out. Scratching her head, she could feel something small and crunchy.

"What?" She said to herself, but when she pulled it back, she laughed a little. "Leaves? What happened last night?" She could hear someone downstairs and the commotion that followed. Realization began to wash over her. "Oh my god, what have I done?!" Jumping from her bed, she padded to the door as fast as she could. Something had happened to Doc, and she couldn't help but feel as if it were all her fault.

"Quick, get Doc to the observation room, Ann. You have to go with them; who knows what that witch did to your eye?" Shelby met the group at the bottom of the stairs. Ann had haphazardly thrown her cloak over the rack as they disappeared down the hall.

"What happened she asked, looking over at Drew, who was holding the little man like a baby. He had wrapped Stardock in Victor's coat, shrouding him from the sun.

"Witches, Shelby. It was the witches." The five of them wandered to the back of the house, through the conservatory, and to the back wall. "What's this?" Drew asked as they all stopped in their tracks.

"The observation room," Ann said as she lifted her hands and closed her good eye. "Aperta Nunc." The wall began to move a little at first, but then it slid open like it was on wheels.

"You're going to have to show me that trick," Shelby said as she walked through the door. They all followed her. The room reminded Andrew of the morgue he and Hunter worked at. Here, he had everything he could possibly need to help his friend.

"Quick, put him on the table!" Victor said, "We haven't another moment to spare." Drew ran over to the table and laid Stardock down, uncovering him.

"Oh my God, what did they do?" Shelby said, covering her mouth with her hands. The poor little man's skin had begun to turn blue. Shelby wasn't sure if he was breathing anymore.

"How much of last night do you remember?" Ann asked as she walked over to Victor, who had begun mixing two liquids in a beaker.

"Not much. I think I was outside, but that's only because I had leaves in my hair."

"You and Doc went to the meadows; Samuel and Keen had gone to find you; if it weren't for Ann's visions when we were on the way to save Victor, I fear Stardock would have been killed." Shelby's eyes widened in shock.

"But why, why would I have gone to the meadows?"

"Misty seems to think you were drawn there by the tree. Said you were talkin' all goofy, calling yourself this um... Hold on; I wrote it down somewhere 'cause it sounded important or made up." The sound of the man's voice on the intercom brought comfort to Shelby. She had grown to like Sam.

"What are you doing up there, old man?" Victor yelled as he pulled a bright yellow bud off of one of the plants in the corner and threw it into the beaker. It began to bubble, and the man gave the potion to Ann, who pushed past the others in a heated rush.

"After last night and the flank attack, and with Keen being injured and all, I thought it would be a good idea to check out the sights."

"See anything of importance?" Drew asked, but his mind and attention were on Doc. Ann had grabbed a scalpel and cut a tiny opening where the fairy king had stabbed him the night before, pouring the concoction directly into the open wound. Drew had to fight off the urge to pull her off the halfling because he knew what she was doing was going to help him.

"Ah, here it is... She called herself the Qhizyja." At the sound of the word, Ann almost dropped the beaker, but Drew steadied her hand.

"I don't remember that," Shelby said as she put her hands down by her side.

"No, I don't suppose you would, Shelby. You weren't there when that happened." Ann said. She could tell that the woman had contempt in her voice, but all her attention was focused on helping Doc, as it should be.

"What does that mean, Ann?" Victor asked, walking closer to the others. "Is he going to be okay?" Ann had poured the potion inside the little man and covered his wound with her hand.

"Consano," Ann muttered, and when she lifted her hand from the man's chest, his wound was gone.

"You're just full of surprises, aren't you?" Drew said with a smile, putting a reassuring hand on the woman's shoulder.

"That's all we can do for the time being. I think we made it by the skin of our teeth. I can't help but feel responsible for this, Drew. How could I have been so stupid?"

"We all make mistakes. You're trying to correct yours, and that's what's important now." Drew leaned over and looked at Ann. He could feel her sorrow, and he knew that the fact she had lost an eye hadn't even crossed her mind yet. All her attention was on saving her friend. It was commendable.

"What is that thing? The thing I called myself last night in the meadow. Ann, what happened?" Shelby looked at the woman, confused.

"You called yourself the Goddess of Oracles. You're fulfilling the prophecy, the one where you will raise the army of fairies; you're going to be the end of us all."

"No, no, that can't be right. I wouldn't want to hurt any of you." Victor looked over at Shelby.

"At this point, I don't think it's up to you anymore."

"Hey, I think we have a problem... Well, possibly two." Sam said they could hear the urgency in his voice, so everyone stopped what they were doing to listen to what the gunslinger had to say.

"What is it, Sam?" Drew asked. He looked down at his friend; it seemed the blue was leaving his skin, and a healthy shade of grey was beginning to return.

"Looks like Misty and Keen are bouncing out the back door, but that's the lesser of two evils."

"Spit it out, Sam!" Ann, with a little irritation.

"Well, love, the witches, they're coming from the front."

"Oh no, what do we do?" Shelby asked as she inched towards the dividing wall. Ann walked toward her and pushed her back toward Drew.

"I can't let any of you go out there; I can't risk any of you getting hurt, not again." Running through the open wall, Ann lifted her hand once again, and before any of them had a chance to advance, she yelled the words that would seal them inside the tomb. "CLAUDE OSTIUM." The three that were left on the other side watched in disbelief as the wall slid shut as quickly as it had opened.

"Well, shit. What do we do now?" Drew said. He had begun to pace the room as Stardock started to move a bit on the table.

"She's right," Victor said, sitting down on a metal chair and putting his head in his hands.

"About what?" Shelby asked.

"If anyone can stop them, it would probably be her." Putting a finger in the air, Drew tilted his head a little and looked up.

"Let's not forget about Lark... Or should I say Mercy."

CHAPTER THIRTY-FIVE

Samuel ran from the top of the stairs; faster than lightning, he was tearing through the foyer and to the back of the house like a cat at three in the morning. He had to get to Misty and Keen. What had caused them to bolt as they did? The last time he saw them, they were making their way to the yellow beater. Probably to get the flowers she had picked the night before. What was so important about them anyway?

"Hey, yawl, I would advise you to get the hell back in the house. We got some pretty nasty company on the way from the ridge." Misty had pulled the coat hood up and over her head, hiding her face from the sun. Samuel had learned from Drew's mistake and locked the car down before they got into the house, but that hadn't stopped Keen from busting the window open with one meaty punch.

"You leave now; we go now," Keen said. Misty had paid the gunslinger no mind and was rummaging through the back seat.

"Ah, here it is." She said as she pulled the satchel and the wand out from under the seat. She had thought it a good idea to put it there for safekeeping. She didn't want too many people asking questions; it wouldn't be good for morale.

"Didn't you hear what I said, little missy?" Turning to face the man, Misty smiled her snake-like smile and took a step closer to Sam.

"The name's not Missy, it's Misty... Misty Lancaster." Samuel's eyes widened as he saw her face and looked over at her arm. The blades on the ends of her fingers had grown longer, and the skin on her arm was the foul shade of grey like the fairies.

"Oh, my darlin', what happened to you?" Sam took a step back and put a shaky hand against one of his pistols. Misty's smile got even more sinister as she continued to walk closer to the man.

"You're welcome to try and shoot me, cowboy, but at the end of the day, one of us is going to take you out. Is today a good day to die, old man?" Samuel knew that the girl was right, but he had to try and stop them. She was clearly going back to the meadow because he knew by the looks of the wand in her hand, she was going to bring back Mara Lafea. Pulling the gun from its holster, he pointed it straight at the girl, who began to giggle. "I love a good fight." Motioning for Keen to help, the giant ogre of a man let out a battle cry, and even though Sam shot his last round squarely into the man's chest, he was unaverted from his attack.

"We go NOW!" Keen yelled as he threw a strong left hook at Sam's face, throwing him onto the ground. Misty could hear growling from the other side of the car and knew it had to be that annoying police dog they felt so obliged to bring along.

Lifting his foot high in the air, Keen let out another yell, stomping at the ground, trying his best to crush the gunslinger, but the man was too fast for Keen, even when he was lying on the ground. "Die, die, DIE!" Keen growled, and so did the dog as it made its way around the car, staring directly at Misty, who had her human hand out in front of her like a shield.

"Good doggie, nice doggie." She began, but it advanced on her, biting her on the ankle. Falling to the ground, Misty screamed, and the sound of his fallen companion caused Keen's attention to return to her.

"NO, bad dog." He said as he lumbered over to Misty, picking her up and throwing her over his shoulder. Swatting at the dog with his free hand, it began to snap and growl at Keen. "We go now," Keen said in a somber tone, paying the bloodhound no more attention and lumbering off into the woods behind the cabin. The dog ran to Samuel's side, licking him on the face. He could feel the bruise on his chin begin to swell and knew he would be lucky if it weren't broken.

Getting to his feet, Samuel gave the dog a little pat on the head.

"Thanks, partner, you were a big help back there. Looking at the beast's collar, he shook his head. "I think we can give you a better name than 1977... How about Champ?" The dog barked once, and Sam smiled a painful smile. "Well, Champ, I think we'd best mosey back into the house. Troubles a Brewin' right on the other side of that their ridge, and I bet you're hungry."

CHAPTER THIRTY-SIX

Hunter laid in bed beside Lark. Her head was on his shoulder, and her hand over his heart protectively. The entire time they were together, Hunter felt electrified, almost superhuman. How did he get to be the luckiest and unluckiest man all at the same time? He didn't know but wouldn't change it for the world.

Lark had fallen asleep, bathed in the glow of the sun that had washed through the whole room like a tidal wave of hope. She was magnificent, a pure beauty. Hunter ran his hand down the curvature of her body and wanted nothing more than to take her away from the danger and uncertainty that was to follow. Lark had slipped on Hunter's shirt and wore nothing more than her underwear. He, himself, had put on his pants, but just because common sense knew he would probably need to leave in a hurry if something was to go down.

Stirring from her slumber, her eyes fluttered open and landed on Hunter's flushed face. The afterglow was still burning, and the contentment on his face made her smile genuinely.

"I fell asleep, didn't I?" She said, rubbing the slumber from her face.

"Only for a moment," Hunter responded as he placed a kiss on her forehead. Getting out from under the covers, Hunter reached under the bed and slipped on his shoes. "Aren't you going to get dressed? It's been far too quiet in the house. I get concerned when it's too quiet." Sitting up in the bed, she looked down at the ratty old tee she had on and hugged herself.

"Why would I? This shirt smells like you, and it makes me happy." But that was the last thing she said before a wave of dizziness hit her, and she fell backward, her head landing on the soft goose-down pillow.

"Lark?" Hunter asked as he climbed across the bed, but knew in an instant what was happening. Her short, knotted hair began to grow, turning into crimson locks that curled wild like forest vines. Her skin took on the blue of the Moon-shadow flower, and she began to grow taller. The tee was, once far too big for her, began to shrink.

Hunter got to his feet and began to back away from the woman. It was harder this time to watch her slip away because, for some reason, he believed she had taken a piece of himself with her. "Goodbye, Lark," He whispered as the new person in front of him sat up with a start. Mercy looked over at the man and nodded. Getting up out of bed, she spent no time with formalities, ripping the shirt from her body and throwing it at Hunter, who quickly put it on.

"We must hurry," Mercy began as she slipped the dress over her head, letting the silky gown slide down her perfectly formed frame. Most men would have preferred her this way, tall and curvy with perfect silk locks and piercing eyes, but not Hunter. He yearned for the day he would get to see his mousy, awkward, perfectly perfect Lark once again. The hope that the day would arrive was all that Hunter could cling to. If he lost that, he would surely die of a broken heart.

"What is it, Mercy?" Hunter asked as he began to hear the commotion beneath them.

"My sisters are here. They want to take me to the door. They have the Mother's Heart. Ann must have taken it while I was out."

"The Mother's Heart? Do you mean that weird necklace Shelby found in the cave?" Mercy pointed to the door and nodded.

"It's not just a necklace, and you know it. It's a key, and everyone has a reason for wanting it."

CHAPTER THIRTY-SEVEN

"How are we going to get out of here?" Shelby said as she began to pace the observation room, a look of trepidation spreading across her face.

"Don't look at me; Ann has the words and the magic to open the wall," Victor said with a groan, running a meaty hand through his grey hair. Andrew's attention was still drawn to Stardock. His concern for the little man-made Victor like him even more. It had been a long time since he had seen compassion for fairy folk. "He must have made an impression on you, huh, Drew." The sound of his name stirred him from the sleeping halfling.

"Yes, he did. I can see a lot of myself in his actions. We are both alone in this world, and the family we have now, we made. I can't give up on him... I won't." It was commendable how Andrew felt. Victor could easily see why his people turned to him for help.

"We aren't doing him or anyone else any good in here, though," Shelby said as she continued to pace.

"No, we aren't." Victor agreed, "But Ann wanted to protect us, and you have to understand something about her, Shelby. She can see things... Things we can't."

"She can see things." Shelby said mockingly, "Again, I ask you, what's so friggin' special about her? She's just another one of... Them."

"Them? Who's them?" Drew asked, but his attention was turned back to Stardock, who began to moan. He opened and closed his hands and began to shake his head back and forth like he was having a bad dream. "Doc? Doc! It's us. We need you; can you wake up?"

"No, I can... I can see them. They are coming. The door. The DOOR!" Stardock sat upright on the table and looked over at Drew. At first, he had a look of fear on his face, but then he threw his arms around the man, almost making the fedora fly off his head.

"Wow," Drew said with a laugh, putting a reassuring arm around the halfling. Pulling away from the man, Doc looked over at Victor.

"The witches," Doc began, but the large man put a hand up and nodded.

"We already know Doc, but Ann, she locked us in here." Taking a look around the room and shaking his head, he understood why.

"Well, that would make sense. We don't need her out there... Not right now. She must have seen it, too."

"Seen what exactly?" Shelby said bluntly. Stardock could tell that the woman was going manic again. He hated it when she became manic. "Well, spill it out; you're talking about me, right? Don't I have the right to know what's going on? Or is that something for SPECIAL Ann to know?" Her concern for the halfling had all but vanished from sight.

"Shell, what's wrong with you?" Drew asked as he took a step closer, but Stardock grabbed his shoulder.

"I wouldn't get too close; she could pop at any moment." Looking back at the little man, Drew had so many questions, but the halfling was clearly frightened, his pointy ears drooping, his eyes focused on his feet rather than anyone in the room.

"Why don't you come over here and sit with me?" Victor said, pointing to another metal chair, but Shelby shook her head. She had the oddest look on her face and had begun to scratch at her wounds.

"Well, Doc? Enlighten the class." She said again, taking a threatening step towards him.

"Hey!" Drew commanded as he put a protective hand up and in front of her. Shelby just looked around it with that same creepy face and focused all her attention on Doc.

"Wait, don't... Don't hurt my friends." Stardock said with a whimper. "I know what you want me to say. I've known for quite a while."

"What is it, Doc?" Victor asked. Shelby let out a laugh as she continued to scratch at her legs. Small trickles of blood began to form on her pants, and Drew thought that he could see something protruding from one of the holes, something that looked like a root.

"He's been lying to you all. He's a lying little halfling BASTARD!" She said as she leaped towards Stardock. Drew took the hand that was already out and used it to push the girl back.

"What the hell has gotten into you?!" Drew exclaimed. "He's our friend."

"Speak for yourself," Shelby hissed, and this time, he thought he could see a flash of light cross her eyes, like the lights of his old yellow hooptie. "Tell them, or I will."

"Fine, fine. Victor, we found another resurgence paper... We were wrong about Shelby, about her army. Victor, we were wrong."

"What do you mean by wrong?" Stardock could see the anger flash across his face.

"You see, Coal and I, we were initially looking for information on the witches and stumbled onto something... We didn't think it was relevant at the time."

"And why is that, Doc?" Victor had gotten to his feet. The look of intensity was deadening, and Doc cowered in fear.

"We didn't think she existed then. Our priority was Mercy and the sisters. We were very wrong, Victor, and I would suppose so are the fairies." Shelby let out a giggle, and there was no denying what Drew and Victor saw next. Her legs had begun to sprout; the roots started to slide from the wounds and wrap around her like octopus tentacles. The two of them backed away from the girl; Drew snatched up Doc, holding him like a toddler.

"How wrong are we talking here?" Victor whispered to Doc. They were all pressed against the far wall, crammed together as if they were trying to get into a photo booth.

"Wrong enough, she's going to raise an army, but not the one we thought. The troll fairies are her enemies, which is why she hates me so much. Victor, she's going to raise an army of a whole new type of fairy, one I've never heard of before."

"What are they called, Stardock?" Victor said. He couldn't keep his eyes off the girl, who had now started to float. Her hair waved to the flow of invisible wind at her back.

"The whimsies, the prophecy calls them whimsies."

CHAPTER THIRTY-EIGHT

Ann and Samuel were standing at the door when Hunter came running down.

"What are you doing??" Ann barked, "You can't be here, not now, and Mercy isn't ready."

"She looked ready enough to me!" Hunter said as he ran past them, grabbing Sam by the wrist as he went.

"Wow, what are you doing, partner?" He said as he began to resist. Hunter stopped, but only for a second,

"Trust me, you don't want to be here for this catfight." For some reason, the gunslinger knew that Hunter was right and allowed him to usher the man down the hall and into the conservatory with Champ at their heels.

The front door began to shake, and then it was blown off its hinges; standing right on the other side were the two wicked sisters, Merry Belle and Melinda, ready to take what was theirs.

"I see you've come to give me back my necklace," Ann said as she pointed at Merry Belle's neck. It was covering the deep scars that Ann had given her a few hours before. They could heal quickly, but it took some time for the scars to fade.

"Sure," Merry hissed, her red lips turned up into a menacing sort of smile. Winking at Ann, she took a step inside of the house. "Maybe while I'm at it, I'll give you back your eye too." Melinda let out a laugh and walked past her sister; Ann had harnessed the fairies' powers once again, allowing her arms to turn a vivid shade of grey, her black nails growing by the second. Sharp razor fangs began to form in her mouth, her tongue forking. Leaning back, ready for the attack, Ann stood in wait. Instead of attacking, though, the witch pulled a small crystal ball and placed it on the table in the middle of the foyer.

"I'm sure you're aware of what happened to your friend, right, Ann?" Then the woman pulled out something else: something far more macabre, Coal's tongue.

"Oh my God," Ann said, recoiling a little at the sight.

"What?" Melinda said as she walked back towards her sister. "I did that for you, I did that for Victor... That vile little man has been keeping secrets from you both." Ann was unfazed by the words that came out of the witch's mouth.

"I don't believe you, Melinda."

"You don't have to; no one has to get hurt. We just want our sister." Melinda pointed up at the ceiling. "Go on, call her. I can feel her presence. She's right there."

"And if I don't?" Ann said, raising her hands, ready to advance.

"Then we will take her by force." Merry Belle said. The evil in her voice dripped off of her words like honey laced with arsenic. No wonder she could control the humans; she was almost irresistible to Ann. Running towards the girls, Ann reached out to claw at them, but Melina snapped her fingers, and Ann flew across the room like a paper airplane, landing hard on her back and sliding across the finished hardwood floor. Letting out a hard oof as she hit. Stars began to dance around her head; she hadn't taken a hit like that in years. The witches had grown increasingly powerful over the years. Ann wasn't sure if she could take them on alone.

"Why don't you try that on me?" Mercy said as she began to descend the stairs, running her red fingernail down the top of the banister, allowing little splinters to rise.

"Sister." Merry Belle said with a smile, raising her hands towards her as if she were going to embrace Mercy.

"Do you honestly think I am a fool? I am not the same girl that you left with the Witch Doctor Melinda, and I know why you've come."

"Well then," Merry Belle said, "let us be on with it." Making a waving motion with her hands, Merry Belle lifted Mercy off the steps, throwing her violently onto the foyer table, causing the ball, the tongue, and a vase full of sunflowers to fly across the room like a parade of color. Rolling over onto her back, Mercy got to her feet, unimpressed. Snapping her fingers, Mercy threw her two sisters out onto the front yard, five yards from the house. Melinda got to her feet, but Merry Belle struggled a little.

"You will leave this place, and you won't come back. Do you hear me?" Mercy said matter-of-factly. Melinda sneered at her little sister's audacity.

"No, you have to help us; we need you at the door; you're the only one that can stop him. Luckily for you, though, you can do it dead or alive." Grabbing one of her own fingers, Melinda pulled it back until it snapped. Mercy screamed in pain, looking down at her arm. The bone had begun to break through the skin. Merry Belle had finally gotten to her feet; Mercy used the opportunity and raised her good hand.

"Avolare!" Merry Belle felt the necklace fly off her neck and into the brush. Grabbing at her neck, Mercy could see the panic in her eyes.

"No! We have to find the key; we can't open the door without the key!" Merry Belle began to walk towards the brush but stopped when she heard what Mercy said next.

"All this talk of taking things, things that one doesn't respect... I think I might take something of yours, something your father gave to you... Something you never wanted."

"No!" Melinda screamed as she grabbed another one of her fingers, but this time, Mercy was at the ready.

"Ligare Et Tacere," Mercy said, and Melinda fell to the ground, unable to move or speak. "I know she will be up soon, seeing as I'm only just now growing into my powers, but before she does, I will have finished with you." Walking across the yard, Mercy grabbed Merry Belle by the throat so tightly that she couldn't speak. Lifting her from the soft grass, Mercy looked at her sister, her eyes glistening in the sun. "Merry Belle, I take your gift, the eternal youth your father bestowed on you, because you used it vainly and cruelly, and you hurt my friends." Letting go of the woman, she fell to the ground, and right in front of Mercy's eyes, she watched Merry Belle as she began to age. Seventy-one years, to be exact. Now old and frail, the magicless old lady looked up at her from the ground.

"Who are you?" Merry Belle screeched as she put a wrinkled hand up to shield herself from the sun.

"I'm your sister. Don't you remember Merry Belle?" The slits on her wrists from all those years ago began to open, fresh red blood, as red as Merry Belle's now milky white hair used to be.

"What's happening? Who's Merry Belle? I'm Mary, just... Mary." The old hag laid down in the yard by the edge of the brush. Kneeling beside her sister, Mercy scooped her head up in her arms and watched as Mary took her last breath on this plane.

"LIGARE ET RECUPERARE SEQUITUR!" The words from behind Mercy made her fall to the ground beside her dead sister. "How dare you bind me, sister!" The necklace floated up from the brush and landed around Melinda's neck. "Now we will do this the hard way, you MURDERER!" Grabbing the bound woman by the ankles, Melinda vanished into the forest with Mercy hellbent on destroying her father and the curse that came with his bloodline.

CHAPTER THIRTY-NINE

Hunter and Samuel could hear the commotion from the foyer, but Hunter knew that the sisters were more powerful than the two men.

"What can we do?" Samuel asked, instinctively putting his hands on his guns. He knew that he was out of ammo, but the feel of the cold steel against his hands was comforting in a way. If he could just get to his room, he had another box of bullets lying out on the bedside table. They were the normal kind, not the pop goes the fairy kind, but they would do in a pinch, and Sam figured these were pinchy type of days.

"I have faith that Mercy and Ann can take care of themselves." The words slipped out of Hunter's mouth, but he didn't believe a single letter in that sentence. Sam could tell he was just trying to make himself feel better about the situation, but didn't want to point it out. He had never been in love before, but Samuel supposed it would be a nuisance. Always worrying about someone else. Hell, he had to worry enough about his own skin.

Champ had walked over to the wall at the back of the conservatory. He had begun to scratch at it and wince a little.

"Don't worry, boy, you can go outside soon enough," Sam said as he walked over to the wall, but then he stopped and put a hand on it. "Hunter, I think there is someone back there." Walking over to the wall, Hunter put an ear against it and listened for a second.

"Someone's. Sounds like Victor and someone else are talking. I would say Shelby, but it's... It's not." Suddenly, the wall began to shake, causing dust from thc top shelves where the old, forgotten books sat to dance through the air and onto the men's shoulders. Taken off guard, they looked at each other, but this time, it was Samuels's turn to grab Hunter by the arm and drag him back away from the wall.

"I don't know about you, partner, but I'm thinking we might have been safer out there with the girls," Sam said as he whistled for the dog to come to him. The wall began to crack, and roots began to slip through the opening.

"What the hell is going on??" Hunter said. He would have been more frightened by the odd sight, but he had seen enough weirdness to last him a lifetime.

"It's her!" Samuel said, taking a step forward. "It's the Goddess of Oracles!" Hunter could see the disbelief, but the giddiness on the man's face. What did he know? Had he been hiding something from the others? Something vitally important? Hunter thought yes. Backing away towards the door, Hunter watched as the roots tore the wall apart piece by piece. There was a blinding white light, and then she was gone. Victor, Drew, and Stardock were left on the far side of the wall, cowering, but alright.

"What the hell happened!" Hunter asked, torn by what was happening in the room with his friends and what could be happening on the other side of the house with his lover.

"Shelby, she's going after the door. She's finding courage and her army for the war." Doc began. He opened his mouth to say something else, but Samuel stopped him by putting a single finger in the air.

"Well, then, we have to stop her. It's the right thing to do." And just like when Hunter had spoken before, Samuel heard the words come out of his mouth, but didn't believe a single letter in the sentence. He thought, though, that he might have done a better job at his lie than Hunter had because if he hadn't, there was no way they would let him leave the house with them.

The five men walked out of the room together, and Andrew couldn't help but get the feeling of deja vu. How did things like this come full circle? He couldn't lose anyone else; he didn't have the strength. They met up with Ann, who was still getting to her feet. The sunflowers that were once in a vase on the table scattered across the floor like a barrier.

"Could someone please pick those up?" She asked. Andrew ran to her side and took her hand. He helped her steady and looked at her face in wonderment.

"Ann, your eye."

"I know I know; I should get a patch..." But she was cut off by Drew, who threw his arms around the woman. Taken a little by surprise, it took her a moment to hug the man back. "What's gotten into you?"

"Your eye, it's back! A little different, but it's there nonetheless." In a twist of irony, the crystal ball had helped after all. No one could know for sure if it was the convergence of the two witch powers or if it was the last good thing Coal did before he left the world, but the ball that was once on the floor had become a new eye for Ann. Drew thought it made her look even more striking.

Hunter had ventured out onto the porch. Staring across the yard as Doc began picking up the flowers. Emerging from the dining room, Sam took a moment to climb the steps to his room and retrieve the box of bullets that had been calling his name for the last half hour.

"No..." Hunter said to himself as he stepped further into the yard. "It's not her, it can't be her."

"Hunter?" Drew asked as he let go of Ann and walked past Doc to the front door.

"Could you possibly hurry? I really need to get out of the house. Something is wrong." Ann asked, looking over at Doc.

"Sure, but why can't you just walk out?" Doc had begun to put the flowers on the broken table, for lack of a better place.

"Sure, Doc, then you can dance around in Victor's room. I can't pass through a chain of sunflowers."

"Or buttercups." Victor chimed in. He had stayed back a little, taking in everything. He wanted to see where each person would go first, and for some reason, Samuel didn't sit well with him. Walking through the foyer, the large man made his way up the steps and to Sam's room, where he found him loading his second pistol and sliding it back into its holster. He hardly looked up at the man.

"You know, when I was very small, my father would take me to the Guild's library, and we would go through book after book. Man, some of the things we saw together. Did you know you don't even have to leave your room to have an adventure?" Samuel took a step towards the man, pulling the cuffs from his back pocket. "Yeah, while I was up here, I thought to slide into Misty's room and get these as well."

"What are you doing?" Victor asked. Sam was being weird, and he didn't like it, not one bit.

"Well, could you just put these on for me? Chrome is your color." Victor scoffed and took a step closer to the man, ready to fight if he needed to, but quicker than Victor could blink, Sam had pulled the gun with a smirk and a wink of his eye. Letting out a groan, the man did as he was told. As soon as he was secured to the bed rail, Sam shut the door and holstered his gun. "I'm gonna be honest with you, buddy; I sure as shit thought you were gonna yell for help."

"What good would that have done? You would have put a bullet through one of them, and that would have been on me." Samuel nodded, keeping his distance from the large man. He knew that given half the chance, Victor would wrestle the keys away from the gunslinger, and as good a shot as he was, Victor was a better fighter.

"It was on a spring day, not unlike this one, when my father and I stumbled onto the last page of the second resurgence prophecy... The one that your little team so conveniently didn't bother looking for. They all took the Southpaw lineage story and ran with the actual idea that she was going to lead an army of troll fairies against the world?" Samuel let out a hardy laugh and ran a hand across his five o'clock shadow.

In the light of the midday sun, Victor couldn't help but see Buck standing in front of him; from all the photos he had seen, they were the spitting image of each other. Sometimes, Victor wondered what it would have been like to get to meet the man. He was a legend in his own right, and instead of giving his only son his legacy name, he chose to name him after the boy who helped him fight fairies –a fast, loyal friend–the one who chose purity and love over his own life.

"Well, why don't you enlighten me then, Sam? You seem to have it all figured out." Samuel knew the man was baiting him, but couldn't resist telling the cliff notes version of what the paper had to say.

"Fine, but when I go around telling you I told ya' so, you can't get too upset." Victor nodded, "She's going to bring back the superior race, one that we've never seen before, and I'm, no, WE were pretty sure that these new beings were meant to improve our world. My father and I stuck the page in an old dusty book in the back of the guild, and that's where it stayed until..."

"Until Doc and Coal stumbled across it."

CHAPTER FORTY

Melinda continued to drag her sister across the grass. Mercy couldn't do anything but lie there on her back, trying with all her might to break the spell her sister had put on her. The pain from her broken arm felt like fire under her skin, but she knew that it had already begun to heal. She knew after a while that Melinda's powers trumped her own, and there was no way she was going to break free, at least not in this form.

"You killed her. I didn't think you had it in you, but you actually killed Merry Belle." Melinda stopped in a clearing far enough from the house that they couldn't be seen. "I was going to let you live, let you make the choice. You did, after all, survive the nothing, my void of sorrows. You deserved a better chance than that." Dropping Mercy's foot, she reached up and touched the necklace that was pressed against her collarbone. It complemented her in every way, like it was made just for the beautiful, pouty-lipped beauty standing before Mercy. Sticks and brush had begun to get caught in Mercy's hair like a wreath of shame. She tried again to open her mouth and to speak, but she couldn't. Closing her eyes, she began to will Lark back from the abyss, but it did not work. "No, I fear now I have to avenge my sister. So, I'm going to kill you and open the door to the mirror world just long enough to throw your corpse inside, and then the curse will be over. If I smash the crystal, he can't come for me. He will be locked away forever."

Reaching up to the heavens, Melinda began to chant. Mercy could feel the bones inside her body begin to bend unnaturally. The pressure was unimaginable.

'Please,' Mercy thought to herself, 'If you ever want to see your lover again, you have to come back... You have to come back NOW!' As Melinda continued to chant, Mercy began to feel her body change, becoming smaller and frailer, and as soon as the transformation was complete, she was released from the binding spell. Trying to get to her feet, she began to scream.

"HUNTER!" Melinda stopped her chant for a second as she saw Lark get to her feet.

"Oh no, you don't." She said as she grabbed the little woman by her broken arm and threw her onto the ground.

"Well, what do we have here? A sisterly quarrel?" The voice from behind her made Melinda recoil with disgust. Pointing at the cowering girl, Melinda grinned an evil grin and said a single word."

"Crura." And just like that, her legs went numb. She couldn't stand, let alone run away from the three evils that stood before her.

"It's you again," Melinda said, turning her sights towards Misty.

"Yeah, thought I would let the three of you take each other out. I couldn't go too far, though, since Deaththorne really wants that necklace. Hell, I kind of want it too. Mirror world sounds like a wild ride." Misty began to pace the edge of the clearing, her one-taloned hand ready to strike.

"Do you really think you can just take the stone from me?" Melinda asked as she took a step closer to the beastly woman.

"No, but I was told if I found you again to kill you. Haven't gotten to do a whole hell of that in a while. I'm up for the challenge." Leaping towards the witch, Misty swung with her fairy arm, barely missing the woman's face. Holding out her hand, Melinda opened her mouth to speak, but before she could, Keen stomped towards her, swatting the woman hard across the face with his open hand.

"NO!" He roared, "Bad witch!" Melinda could hear ringing in her ears. Her vision had begun to double; stumbling to the side, she fell hard, tripping over Lark. Misty walked over to Melinda, snatching her by the neck, slicing her throat with a long, sharp, black nail. Grabbing at her neck, the woman began to cough and choke on the blood that was now spurting out of her corraded artery with every beat of her heart. Taking the necklace from around the witch's neck, Misty grinned. Lark couldn't move; she couldn't speak either, not from the spell but from the sheer terror of it all. Blood had sprayed her face and dress. She looked like the final girl in a horror movie, and that was exactly how she felt.

"Hmm," Misty said as she slipped the Mother's Heart into her pants pocket. "I believe I heard somewhere that your type really likes to heal fast. Let's do a little experiment. How fast can you heal from this?" Walking towards the choking woman, Misty lifted Melinda's head in her hands. Opening her mouth wide, her jaw unhinging just like a snake, exposing sharp yellow teeth, Misty stuck Melinda's head inside of her mouth and, with a loud crunch, took it clean off of the witch's shoulders. Keen jumped up and down with glee, clapping his hands and laughing.

"Again, again!" He said in excitement. Getting to her feet and letting the corpse of the woman fall to the ground, she tapped her finger against her face, chewing up what was left of her skull. Bits of red hair fell to the ground like collateral damage.

"She tasted like... Revenge." Lark looked up at her saviors and her captors; she didn't know what to do. As soon as her sister took her last breath, the spell had begun to wear off, and Lark had started to yell inside her head for Mercy to return, but she wouldn't. "What should we do with the little one?" Misty hissed, kneeling over her and wiping a bit of blood from Lark's eyes.

"Please... Please, I don't wish you any harm. I don't want the necklace. I just want to go home." Lark pleaded. Her sadness and fear made Misty even happier. She thought for a moment about just keeping the girl alive for her own amusement, but thought better of it.

"I can't do that. You're one of them." Misty pointed over to the corpse and tilted her head.

"But I killed my other sister. I'm not like them. I swear." Misty lifted her head, looking at her tall friend with mischievous eyes.

"What do you think? Should we let her go?" Keen stopped and looked down at the helpless woman on the ground. What was left of the real man screamed behind the bars of his mind, trapped like a rat inside a maze. He couldn't escape.

"I smash, little bird," Keen said with a grin.

"Smash away, big guy," Misty said as she walked to the other side of the clearing, facing the house. Keen stomped over to the woman, his eyes dull and lifeless, like a zombie. With a sideways smile, he lifted a big foot but was stopped by the sound of a gun cocking. Looking up, Misty saw the gunslinger; he was pointing the gun at Keen's head.

"Now, what are yall doing out here? I thought you would be on your way out." Keen began to lower his foot towards Lark's head, but Sam shook his head. "Hey there, little guy, I know the first bullet didn't take you out, but a headshot sure as shit will. Or maybe you would rather me pop one in your little girl over there." Turning the gun on Misty did the trick. Backing away from Lark, the giant ran with surprising speed toward Misty, picking her up and throwing her over his shoulders.

"No! Bad Man!" He yelled as they both vanished through the woods once again. Holstering his gun, he knelt by the girl and got her to her feet. She was struggling to walk barefoot, so he eventually picked her up.

"Come on." He said, looking at the bloody girl. "There's a man right over the hill, beside himself with grief. We should probably get you home." Home, what did that even mean anymore?The one thing that she did know was that when she found it, she would be in Hunter's arms, because nowhere would feel right without him.

CHAPTER FORTY-ONE

"No, it can't be her... It's not her." Hunter said as he made his way towards the frail porcelain frame lying at the edge of the brush. Samuel had pushed past the heartbroken fellow. Something told him to go further into the forest. He had always had a knack for those sorts of things. With Victor bound, gagged, and locked safely out of sight, he felt hope that his plans would fall into place.

"Hunter, please come back to the house," Drew said as he began to follow the man. He didn't know what to do, and with the witches and now the

Qhizyja freed, there was danger all around. Hunter couldn't take the suspense any longer and sprinted towards the body. Crying out in fear and confusion. He scooped her lifeless corpse off the ground and stared at her old, ragged face. Who was this? Could this be Lark? He studied her shape. She was small and thin, but her hair had turned white; she had aged fifty years.

Ann had emerged from the foyer and made her way to Hunter's side. Putting a gingered hand on the man's shoulder, she looked down and smiled.

"It's not her Hunter."

"How do you know?" He asked shakily. His whole body trembled with trepidation. Ann pointed down to the woman's neck; there, like a badge, stood four thin scars.

"I put those there last night. The woman you're holding is Merry Belle Monroe." Letting out a sigh of relief, he let the old lady fall to the ground and got to his feet, looking into the distance.

"Where did she go? What happened?" Hunter began to walk toward the wooded entrance, but let out a laugh of joy when Sam emerged from the brush moments later with Lark in his arms. Hunter scooped her up and made his way back to the house. She wrapped her good arm around the man and kissed his cheek. Tears of relief began to fill Hunter's eyes, and he felt no shame in them.

"Lark, your arm," Drew said as they walked inside. "We should cast it." Hunter nodded, and they made their way to the conservatory, back to the open wall. There, they would have all they needed.

Samuel and Ann walked across the field back to the house.

"Are you going to tell me what happened, Sam?" She spoke. Looking over at the woman, he began to assess what she meant by the comment and concluded she meant it about Lark, not Victor.

"I did the best I could, I really did, but Lark told me that Misty got the Mother's Heart, and if I'm correct... I feel that I am on this one; she's going to open the door."

"Deaththorne? You suppose he enlisted her to bring back Mara, don't you?" Sam nodded at Ann.

"You know I'm right. She's on foot; if we take the car, we can beat her to the meadows." They made their way inside the house, and Ann turned to shut the door when the realization hit that they didn't have one anymore.

"What about the other sister?" Ann asked, but Sam shook his head.

"Dead... Thinking, Misty bit off her head. It would have been epic to see." Ann cocked her head at the comment but let it slide since Sam was a battle-hardened type of guy, just as his father had been before him.

"Have you two seen Victor?" Stardock asked as he emerged from the dining room. He had discarded the flowers into the trash. "I've been looking for him, but he's nowhere to be found." Samuel knew that he had to think on his feet. He was so close to utopia; he didn't want to lose it now.

"He went upstairs, something you said to him on the wall, I suppose. Said he had something to look into. I wouldn't bother him right now." Doc opened his mouth to say something and then shut it again, taking the man's words as facts. He did, after all, drop the bomb that Shelby was raising a new army and that they all knew very little about who or what they were. It would only make sense that he would try to find out about these people and what they were about.

"We have to get the guys; we have to get to the meadows before they do, and wherever that necklace is, Shelby will follow." Ann motioned for them to get to the back of the house quickly. The two men had begun to set Lark's arm when Ann, Doc, and Samuel walked through the wall.

"We have to act fast if we want to get the upper hand on this." Samuel began. "We need to get the car, and we need to go to the meadow. Misty has the stone." Drew looked over at the trio by the hole and nodded.

"I agree, but how do we stop an unstoppable force?"

"With magic," Ann said, crossing her arms. "I have a trick or two up my sleeve."

"No, you can't go back there. I can't go back there, no... Not to the door." Lark began to mumble. "My father, he could be waiting for me." Hunter nodded, putting a protective arm around the woman's shoulder.

"It's not safe for her." But before Hunter had a chance to say another word, Lark began to grow.

Her hair got longer, and her bloody dress began to fill out with the curves and lengths of her body. Lark had vanished once again, and in her place sat Mercy.

"I have to do as she asks," Mercy said, pulling away from Andrew and removing the splint from her arm. "Hunter, I have to go now. I will give you the choice. You can stay here and fight alongside your friends. It would be commendable to do so, but you will lose her forever." Hunter thought for a moment and looked over at his friends.

"I have to leave Drew. I will find you all again, but for now, I have to go with Mercy." Drew nodded in agreement, and with a single movement of her arm, Mercy and Hunter vanished from the room in a poof of blue dust.

"Do you think we will see them again?" Doc asked; Drew could see the disappointment in the little man's eyes.

"Knowing Hunter? I can absolutely count on it." Drew responded, putting a hand on his friend's shoulder.

"I hate to break this up," Samuel said as he grabbed Ann by the shoulder. "But we really have to go. Time is on our side, but not for long." Ann nodded as they made their way out of the room and back through the house.

"Wait, shouldn't we get Victor?" Doc asked as they made their way outside. Stardock grabbed the discarded cloak on the rack by the front of the steps and followed the others onto the front lawn.

Drew could see the shattered window as soon as they got to the car.

"Damnit!" He said, scratching his head. "Who the hell did that!"

"I'll give you one guess." Sam retorted, opening the front door and ushering Ann inside. "Do you have the keys?" Drew nodded and pulled them out of his coat pocket, getting into the driver's seat.

"Victor..." Doc began, but Sam grabbed the little man and basically threw him in the back, pushing him across the seat as he, himself, got in beside the halfling.

"There's no time, we have to go now." Putting the key into the ignition, the yellow beater sprang to life. Drew thought that the squeal had gotten worse, but didn't say anything about it. Riding down the mountainside, they all made it through town before the car took its final steps and puttered out on the side of the road near the Dodson Hotel.

"Shit, what do we do now?" Drew said, punching the steering wheel. "Hunter was better working on this thing than I ever was." Ann could see the hurt in her friend's eyes. Even though he understood Hunter's decision, it still broke his heart that he may never see him again. Under the same circumstances, though, Drew probably would have done the same thing.

"We're still gaining on 'em," Sam said as he got out of the car, pulling Doc with him. "I guess we're hoofing it."

"But Sam, the sun..." Doc began, but once more, the gunslinger didn't want to hear what the halfling had to say. Samuel's constant flippant behavior towards Stardock was proving to put the little man in a foul mood. Drew could tell right away and got out of the car.

"I hate to point out the obvious here, but we have to. Everyone's future is at stake, but if you feel a little too exposed, you're more than welcome to use my coat as well." Stardock looked over at the man and smiled. With every passing day, he had become increasingly fonder of him. Getting out of the car, Ann motioned for them to follow her. Lifting a hand in the air, she waved it in a circle, causing a little tsunami of ripples all around her. Within seconds, the pink lady didn't look pink anymore. She had tan skin and curly brown hair. The only thing that gave her away was her eyes; one had remained blue, but the other one was crystalline white and sparkled in the sun like a diamond.

"Well, hot damn, who knew you could do that!" Samuel said as they began their walk down the road.

"I told you, I have a few tricks up my sleeve," Ann said, leading the charge. "Now, let's finish this thing once and for all."

CHAPTER FORTY-TWO

It was nearing dark when Misty and Keen reached the bottom of the mountain. The trek down was slightly more notorious than first thought. Stopping only for a short while at the mouth of the cave, the two of them managed to make good time. Standing in front of the door, Misty looked down at the necklace and then over at her partner in crime.

"Hell, I reckon I lucked out and stumbled onto the door. Who's for starting some shit and getting that fairy queen here?" Keen kicked the dirt all around him, his beefy hands in his pockets.

"Maybe. Maybe we go now." Keen muttered, looking off into the distance at the sunset. The deep purples and pinks cast ominous shadows around the surrounding towns. How many people lived in each one, and how many of them knew of the horrors that would befall them? Misty smiled and put the sack of flowers at the bottom of the door, holding the necklace up to the failing light of evening.

"I thought you were going to let me down," Deaththorne said as he made his way out from the nearby thicket. "I've been waiting in the shadows for you; I would have come for you this very night if you hadn't arrived when you did."

"Ah, old Thorne, looking well, I see," Misty said with a smirk.

"You as well, old friend." Misty could see that the fairy had trouble saying the word friend and she smiled at his uneasiness.

"Friendship is overrated, Thorne; what I crave is power and solitude." Deaththorne made his way to the door and motioned for the girl to put the stone on the divot; she did as she was told. Mere moments later, it cracked open. All she could see was all-consuming darkness, and it gave her chills.

"Go on now, throw in the flowers, give Mara her breadcrumbs so that she can find the correct door." Deaththorne watched in glee as Misty did what she was told, throwing all but one of the Starshallows into the void, leaving the last one on the ground right outside the threshold. "Take her wand and place it by the door. Its light will guide her home." Again, Misty blindly put the wand on the ground, and it began to glow brighter and brighter as the sun finished setting behind Beast Mountain. "Mara, it's Throne, I've come back for you." Misty thought she heard something beginning to emerge from the nothing, and Deaththorne's smile told her she was right.

First, they saw a hand emerge from the nothing and grab the wand from the ground. A pair of piercing eyes looked back at them as the Queen emerged from her own personal hell. She was tall and round, wearing the dress of a noblewoman. Misty couldn't for the life of her understand why the queen looked so... so human.

"Deaththorne." The woman said in a soothing, mother-like voice. "I knew that you would come for me." She took the fairy's hand and planted a kiss on his forehead.

"What have they done to you?" He asked. Mara's long blond hair caught the wind and blew behind her, making the sight even more like a fairy tale.

"It was the last form I took before the banishing. Hope and Faith's mother. I will find a way to fix this, but first, we must feast." Turning her eyes to Misty and Keen, she smiled over at the girl. "There have been stories told about you. Beautiful, dark, and twisted things. They ring about the mirror world, out into the darkness, and into the nothing, your stories speak back. No doubt the reason Deaththorne chose you, and no doubt why you succeeded." Then her gaze turned to Keen, who had refused to look at them directly. "You, though, we have no use for."

"We go now?" Keen said, looking at Misty with pleading eyes.

"Hold on now. That's my big oaf." Misty stood protectively in front of the man, but it did no good. With a wave of her wand, the man began to cough and shake, and within moments, he was on the ground, breathing heavily. Misty could see the light fading from his eyes. It was too late. "You bitch!" She yelled, walking towards them, but Mara held the wand in front of Misty and smirked.

"Give me the necklace, and you may be on your way."

"Yes!" Deaththorne said with glee. He could see the pained look on Misty's face, but knew even in sorrow, the girl couldn't be trusted. She was a trickster, just like him. "We need it to help the Goddess, to help her raise our army. It's been spoken of, and it shall come to pass." Mara took her eyes off Misty long enough to glance at Deaththorne.

"Oh, no, this is to destroy it. You and the others have been misled. The Qhizyja will raise an army, but it will be of another race and another time. She cannot go through the door; she must not find her way back to the Whimsies." Deaththorne went slack-jawed for a moment. Everything that he thought he knew went out the window when she said those words.

"That cannot be; we've read the prophecies. We know."

"Someone stole the last page from everyone: a cowboy and his son. The darkness speaks to me in the mirror world, and it does not lie. Give me the stone NOW!" Mara yelled. The crystal on the end of her wand had begun to glow, foggy mist filling the inside of it, exactly like it had the night Misty had used it against the crazy blond girl. Letting out a laugh, Misty began to back away from the two of them.

"Don't hold your breath, ya old bag!" Misty took off away from the door, holding the Mother's Heart tightly in her fist. Mara screamed out in anger, sending beams of fire through the field, lighting up pockets of dried grass.

"I hope your little door vanishes and you never get what you want! You promised me power, Thorne, and you didn't deliver." Misty leaped behind a large rock, an arrow of fire hitting it square in the middle, leaving a charred spot.

"No, you can't do that!" Mara screamed as she began to walk towards the girl, wand in tow. Getting to her feet, Misty put the necklace back in her pocket and smirked.

"I think I just did." Deaththorne and Mara watched in horror as the cream door began to shake and shimmy, then vanished completely into thin air.

"NOOOOOOOOO!" Mara screamed, running back to the door. "I will never get my form back because of her. I will be hideous forever!" Focusing back on the rock, Mara scanned the field but realized that Misty had vanished into the thicket and that she was more than likely making her way back to the meadow.

Misty hadn't gone very far when she felt a set of glowing eyes on her.

"I may have misjudged you, small one." The voice was familiar and less insane than the first time Misty had encountered her. Looking around, she couldn't see the woman, but she could feel her presence. She was a little on edge but didn't feel threatened this time.

"People tend to do that," Misty said as she continued through the woods. The path that she had chosen was thick and full of thorns.

"I saw what they did back there. They deceived you, and that wasn't fair." Looking around, Misty thought she saw a glimmer of blond hair. Hopefully, it was the Qhizyja and not Mara.

"Yeah, well, in my defense, I was bored at the time." The Goddess let out a little laugh and appeared right in front of Misty as she walked. The roots that had begun to form from her legs had become tamer, along with her temperament.

"Would you like to get even? Would you like to start some chaos with me, Misty?" She thought for a minute, but it didn't take long before a wicked smile crossed her face.

"What did you have in mind?" Misty asked,

"Let's go to the meadows, to the mother tree. Let's open the door and get my army... I cannot promise you magic, but I can give you power in numbers... And these fairies, the Whimsies, they hold great secrets."

CHAPTER FORTY-THREE

The sun had set behind Ann and the others. Stardock had graciously given the cloak back to its rightful owner. Now that she was hooded, Ann had let the spell wear off and looked like her own self again. Approaching the field, Stardock stopped for a moment and then took a gingered step across its borders.

"That's odd," He said as they all began to walk the length of the field, leaving the woods behind them. "I was unable to cross the last time I came here. I was forced to walk around."

"Things seem to change on the daily around these parts," Sam mumbled as he ran his hands across the handles of his guns. Stardock didn't like the way he was acting, watching the gunslinger's eyes dart around the field. He didn't look frightened, no, not to Doc anyway. To Doc, the man looked excited.

"I think I can see the tree up ahead," Ann said as she pointed a long finger directly in front of her, but put it down almost as quickly. "Ouch," Ann said, rubbing her hand. She glanced at the sky with the realization that the moon was at its fullest... A Super moon. "Oh my God." She said as she stopped midstride.

"What is it?" Drew asked, pushing past the others to stand beside her. The look of concern that washed across her face brought serious concern to Andrew's. "What? Ann, you have to tell me." Looking over at the middle-aged man, she didn't know quite how to start.

"The moon..." She began, "Tonight, she's going to open the door because tonight she will be at her most powerful."

"Well, what exactly does that mean?" Drew asked, but ushered her along anyway. Powerful or not, they had to try to stop her; they had to get the necklace and destroy it, because then Andrew could get his friend back, and Lark wouldn't have to hide.

"Aren't you nervous?" Stardock asked, keeping his black marble eyes on the gruff man. The moon illuminated his face, and Doc couldn't help but see

Buck standing beside him. He wore a cowboy hat, always. More than likely, it was because his father did as well, and the mop of brown curls that framed his strong-jawed face made him look younger than he really was. It didn't matter what time of day; he donned a five o'clock shadow, but nothing more than that. Sam with a beard? Never. Tonight, the pensive look that had painted his face reminded Doc mostly of Sam's drive. When he had something on his mind, that was all there was, and he had something big on his mind tonight.

"Fear is subjective. Some use it as a crutch; others use it to define bravery." For the first time that day, Samuel looked over at Doc and smiled at him. That small act of kindness brought back fond memories, flooding the little man with warmth. "How are you going to let it define you, Doc? When it comes down to it?" The halfling thought for a moment and remembered the fight he had with Deaththorne and how strong he felt, slashing the evil King's face.

"I'm going to be brave tonight, Sam. For my friends, I will be brave." Walking over a slight arc in the Field, everyone laid their eyes on the tree. She was magnificent. Her long branches hung low, floating in the wind ever so slightly. The vibrant purple blooms that sprouted across its branches wafted a scent of pure intoxication. A love potion to anyone who dares get too close. The tree seemed illuminated by the moon, which danced above it like a lover longing to be with her once again.

“I can see her.” Doc motioned to the bottom of the tree, and sure enough, there stood Shelby. Her hands up in the sky, distracted by the tree’s ultimate beauty.

“Why hasn’t she opened the door? What is she doing?” Sam asked, still holding the pistols. The question, even though it was a good one, sent a red flag up in Doc’s brain. Did he want her to open the door? If so, then why?

“She has to summon the right door. Unlike the mirror world, where you can pull from any alternative, she has to open the door to another world entirely. One we’ve never seen.” Ann responded, taking a deep breath. She led the others over the arc and closer, still to the Goddess.

“What’s the plan?” Andrew asked; the closer he got to the woman, the more nervous he became. He thought he had an entire beehive inside of his stomach because butterflies were far too tame.

“Keep her distracted, Drew. I need to get to the tree undetected. I have to eat of her fruit.” Samuel could hear the two of them talking and had completely stopped paying mind to Stardock. The halfling was of no consequence. He feared that Ann was the bigger threat. Walking closer to the two of them, he listened to what they were saying very intently. So intently that he didn’t bother seeing Doc wander away from the group. He had to help his friends be brave. That was what he intended to do.

Ann made her way to the side of the tree, a few hundred yards out, while Drew and Sam walked together, closer still, to the Goddess.

"Don't ya ever wonder what it would be like, Drew?"

"What would it be like?" Drew asked, looking over at the gunslinger.

"To live in peace, even if it was just for a little while." Drew nodded, scratching his head. He didn't know how to respond, but he didn' t have to, because Sam had already pulled his weapon. Gun pressed firmly against Andrew's spine; he pushed him closer and closer to the tree and to Drew's ultimate fate.

Hey, Qhizyja, this guy here is trying to stop you from opening the door!" Samuel took his free hand and thumbed at Drew with a grin. Stopping what she was doing, the Goddess smiled and looked at them with two flashlight eyes.

"How do you think you were going to do that? Andrew? Is that your name?" Holding her hand out in a stop motion, a wand made out of a root sprang from her wrist. At the end was an opaque ball filled with white mist. "Ligare et Cecuperare Sequitur." Drew couldn't move, but his body was sliding across the thicket towards the lady. On the other hand, she held the necklace and Earth's last hope at salvation.

Ann watched in horror as her friend was being compelled towards the Qhizyja. She needed a distraction, and Sam unwittingly gave her one. Rushing towards the tree, Ann grabbed the first piece of fruit she saw and bit into it. Its pulp was sweet, the seeds popping in her mouth like bubbles of delight. She had never tasted anything so delicious in all her life... However long that had been.

Behind you, Goddess!" Sam said with wide eyes. Turning around, she came face to face with Ann, but she didn't quite look the same. Floating off the ground, the woman's skin had become purple like the flowers of the tree, her eyes as white as the moon itself, and her hair as black as the night sky.

"So, now it's you, is it? Another one of them!" The Qhizyja began to float, coming face to face with Ann. Even though the girl was wearing ratty old sweats, there was no denying the royalty in her stance. A metallic silver and gold crown slowly formed from the top of her head. "Why is it so hard for people to understand? Your time here is finished. Global reset, it's upon us, and I am in charge!" Holding out her wand, she pointed it at the woman.

"Vis Ager," Ann yelled just before the plasma blast went off in her face. She was thrown back across the field, but her spell kept her from any real harm. Turning around to face Samuel, whose face was filled with glee, she smiled and floated back to the front of the tree, continuing to chant.

"Yes, it's all coming together," Sam said to himself as he walked to the Goddess's side. Stardock squatted in the tall grass, watching from a little distance. He wanted to make sure that the timing was perfect. He watched as Ann got to her feet, as she made her way back to the Willow tree. He wished he had half her determination.

"Whatcha' looking at?" Misty asked as she squatted down beside the halfling.

"You... YOU!" Doc said with a squeak, falling on his butt. Misty let out a little laugh. She loved scaring people. It made her day... Or night in this case.

"Don't worry, ya little booger, I got bigger fish to fry tonight." She pointed over at the Qhizjya. "You see that stone she's got in her hand?" Doc nodded as they began to make their way towards the excitement. "Yeah, well, I've been double-crossed for the last time. Ima' get that shit back. These fairy folk, they love to talk a big game, but they're all the same."

"What do you mean?" Stardock asked. He never thought in a million years he would be working with the likes of Misty. Maybe there was hope for her after all.

"I mean, they wouldn't have been able to pull any of this off without me. I have every right to take it away." Ann was standing in front of the Goddess once again; her hands were balled up into fists, but the Qhizyja just kept chanting. Ann could see the door to the other world begin to form.

The Goddess held out the stone as the vortex inside the tree began to swirl, and the portal opened.

"No!" Ann said as she lifted her hand, but Sam pointed his gun at the Witch with a smirk. Standing in front of his Queen protectively.

"What are you gonna do, Ann? It's over, she's won." The vortex continued to swirl until finally, the door opened, and on the other side was a lush, green forest. She could see a waterfall and hear all the sounds of nature, and just on the other side of the ridge, not unlike a portrait, stood a man... But not just any man, one who looked exactly like Ann.

Her mouth opened in shock as she reached her hand out even further; all the while, Drew continued to struggle; he knew what was about to happen. He wanted to do everything in his power to stop it.

"It's easy to fuck things up when you're counted out," Misty said, appearing beside the Qhizyja, unhinging her jaw, and taking the woman's hand clean off necklace and all. With a scream, the Goddess looked at her hand in rage, but the distraction caused her to let go of the hold she had on Drew. Running towards Ann, he jumped in front of her just in time to catch the bullet that Sam discharged from the gun, hitting him dead in the chest.

Ann grabbed him as he fell to the soft ground, a look of pain across his face.

"What did you go and do that for?" She said with a smile. Drew covered his wound with a tender hand, swallowing hard.

"Figured I hadn't gotten hurt yet. Might as well go out with a bang." Sam looked over at his queen, distracted by her pain. Misty laughed, the hand and necklace still in her mouth. Pointing the gun at the girl, he cocked it, aiming for her head.

"Why do I always have to do things the hard way?" Sam muttered. Putting a finger up in the air, Misty wiggled it back and forth as if to say, 'I wouldn't do that if I were you.' And then bit down hard. The sound of shattering glass echoed through the field, and once again, the Goddess screamed.

"NO!" Samuel said, firing his gun for the second time that night, and his aim would have been true if not for a little man who finally found his bravery. Leaping from the thicket, Doc pushed the two through the vanishing door as the vortex swallowed his friends whole.

Within moments, the tree was exactly as it had been before, standing under the light of the moon undisturbed and untouched by time. Doc sat down, leaning against its roots, taking it all in.

"Is it over?" Drew asked.

"Not quite," Ann responded. The purple in her skin had begun to fade, but she knew she had just enough power for one more spell. Putting her hand over Drew's wounds, she closed her eyes. "Sanitatem Lucem."

CHAPTER FORTY-FOUR

Misty had slipped off into the night, spitting pieces of bone and crystal out of her mouth on the way. She wanted nothing more than to get home and to go to sleep. Even though the sunblock helped, she didn't much fancy the morning rays, and she knew that they would be on their way in a matter of hours.

At first, she thought it was just her paranoia, the fact that she thought she heard a dog barking in the distance, but then she began to feel... Stuck.

"What the hell is going on?" She said to herself.

"Oh, nothing much. You just walked into a fairy trap. Couldn't let you go without saying thank you." Victor walked out of the shadows, Champ at his heels. He had a smile on his face that creeped the girl out.

"But, what... Why?!" She said, looking at the man.

"Because, after I got free, I looked into you. We can't have monsters like you roaming free... It's not natural." Tilting her head at the man, Misty snarled.

"I can't help what the fairies turned me into." Leaning in, he looked the girl square in the eye.

"I wasn't referring to that, Misty Lancaster. You were a monster since the day you were born." That very next morning, Misty was hauled off to the Coral Bay prison, or that's what the newspapers were told. In reality, the Guilds of Magics had a much better place for her type, sitting in a cell beside other magical types, and in this case, she got the cell beside one Mark Randolph.

"Long time no see, Misty." Mark mused as the cell doors shut behind her.

"Hello, uncle. I've been meaning to visit. Started any good apocalypses lately?" Mark let out a little laugh, looking at his kin with a smile.

"No," Mark responded, lying down on his cot.

"Would you like to?"

EPILOGUE

Several weeks had passed since the incident at the meadow. Andrew had been inducted as the newest member of the guilds of magic and partnered up with Stardock. Their first mission? Find the witch.

After what Ann had seen that night, she spent hours inside the conservatory looking through old texts, trying to find all she could on the Whimsies. At least she knew who she was, but she didn't understand the what of it yet.

After his trail of paperwork, explaining to the higher powers what exactly happened and where the gunslinger had vanished, Victor took a little time off, retiring in his two-story townhouse for some well-deserved r and r. He had retired for the evening, falling fast asleep on his king-sized bed, but around three in the morning, something stirred him awake.

Sitting up with a start, the man stared into the full-length mirror. His wife had given it to him the last Christmas she was alive. It was one of the last things he had to remember her by. It had a gold frame with flowers etched into the sides. He knew she had to of spent a pretty penny on it, and he kept it safely tucked away in the corner of his room. He rarely looked into it, but tonight, something told him to; it demanded his attention.

"Victor Zanborn," The voice in the dark called. His reflection began to change, and a tall, thin man in a top hat began to emerge. Victor couldn't make out the man's face. All he could see was an unnatural smile under the enormous hat. "I believe I have something you've been looking for." Getting to his feet, the man walked over to the mirror, touching the glass, but the thing on the other side was not a man.

"What do you want?" Victor fumed, furrowing his brow at the disturbance.

"I want to give you some simple information and then a choice." The smile on the other side of the mirror got bigger and more frightening. Victor took a step back.

"What is it? What have you come to tell me?"The man in the hat tilted his head again, and Victor thought he saw the glint of a reptilian type of eye, green and horrible, just under the brim.

"They tell stories here in the mirror world. Great and horrible things, I quite enjoy. My favorite one as of late is about your family... You see, I am the one who stole them away in the night. I've also been told you want nothing more than revenge. That you heard the cries of your family every night, now that might have been me, possibly, but it might have been you as well." Victor grabbed the sides of the mirror and looked menacingly at the man.

"You!?! You killed them?" Murdock let out a hearty laugh and shook his head. "Who said anything about killing? You might have a chance to get them back... To get your revenge on me as well... But you can do neither if I'm stuck here on the other side of the mirror."

"I'LL KILL YOU!" Victor roared, continuing to shake the mirror. A small crack began to form in the top corner from all the pressure.

"For that, I have no doubt... I'm counting on it."

"How do I get you out? How do I get my hands on you?" Murdock pointed to the bedside table; a journal, with a red pen, had appeared there.

"I need you to write for me, Victor. Thirteen stories. Just write for me."

"Why?" Victor asked, calming down a little and letting go of the mirror. Murdock's smile widened with every waking second.

"Because, my friend, that's how villains are created."

Megan Guilliams is an Independent Fiction author who specializes in Urban Fantasy and Horror. She is a Franklin County native who lives in Virginia with her husband and two children. When she's not writing Young Adult and New Adult Fiction, she enjoys painting. Filling the walls of her home with colorful lowbrow art and Pop art, Megan enjoys bringing her book's characters to life. As a young child, Megan dabbled in short stories, often entertaining her peers. While she doesn't hold any specialized degrees that led her to her writing passion, she currently has over twenty novels published on Amazon and Kindle. You can find more of her work in the year to come, as well as read her story "Kroak" in *Nature Triumphs: A Charity Anthology of Dark Speculative Fiction*, "Love, Lies and Bleeding" in *The Devil's Playground: A Horror Charity Anthology for Drug*

Addiction, "The Christmas Wraith" in *Last Christmas: A Holiday Horror Anthology* and "She Bitch" in *Piece by Piece: An Anti-Valentine's Day Collection of Short Stories, Poetry and Prose.*
https://www.amazon.com/stores/MeganGuilliams/author/B0CTP2D7XD

www.ingramcontent.com/pod-product-compliance
Lightning Source LLC
LaVergne TN
LVHW091022080826
845145LV00002B/326

* 9 7 8 1 9 7 2 5 9 6 0 0 5 *